HOUSE OF SECRETS by Diana Harker

'A deftly-organized, fast moving story going back in time – showing how sombre life can be both in the 21st century and in a Victorian family.'

Gillian Avery – Author of The Warder's Niece

'I loved it! So absorbing and exciting I read it in one go. It has strong elements of an intriguing detective story with vivid characterisation and a real and appealing heorine.'

June Lancelyn-Green – Drama Critic

'This fast moving yet vividly descriptive time-travel adventure with its feisty young heroine and well drawn characters (dramatically contrasted between two eras) is given depth by its hidden message – subtly but tellingly brought home.'

Eileen Dewhurst – Award winning author of 25 novels of detective fiction

By the same author:

Saxon Summer
The Knot Garden
Roman Graffiti

HOUSE OF SECRETS

Diana Harker

Book Guild Publishing
Sussex, England

First published in Great Britain in 2009 by
The Book Guild Ltd
Pavilion View
19 New Road
Brighton, BN1 1UF

Typesetting in Garamond by
SetSystems Ltd, Saffron Walden, Essex

Printed in Great Britain by
Athenaeum Press Ltd, Gateshead

A catalogue record for this book is
available from the British Library

ISBN 978 1 84624 357 8

For Hal, Sophie, Toby, Bede and Ava

Chapter 1

'*Why* can't I come with you?' Jane shouted.

'I've told you how it is,' her mother said wearily, running her hands through her lank fair hair. 'I love you very much, you know that, but I must just have a bit of breathing space and there's this job I might go for – the hotel one in Weston Super Mare . . .'

'But I'll be off school anyway and Billa doesn't want me hanging around – you know we don't get on and—'

'You can't come and that's flat. I've got to have a bit of time to myself. I need to sort things out. *You* know how we're fixed. We always talk everything through, don't we?'

That's just the trouble, Jane thought angrily, if only we didn't. If only she didn't tell me everything with no details spared. 'It's no good sweeping things under the carpet, best to have things out in the open air,' Mum always said but Jane knew that she'd far rather not know all about their financial situation, how Dad, since he'd gone, was bad about paying them any money.

The visits to the Citizens Advice Bureau, Legal Aid, Social Security, the cost of new shoes. Nothing was spared, Jane knew it all. Sometimes she tried not to listen while her mother was telling her yet another grim fact of life, like the cost of renting this horrible poky flat with the damp patches on the thin walls, but she couldn't even get away with this. 'You live in a dream, don't you? You have to wake up and face reality,' Mum said.

Anything was better than the reality. What was wrong with living in a dream where everything was secure, people were happy with no money worries and where she could be allowed to be her own age – twelve – instead of having to pretend to be the same age as her mother, sharing all her problems and fears. Lucky Billa to have escaped to her pharmacy course at Liverpool University.

'You're going to see that man, Stewart, aren't you?' Jane said accusingly; this was another worry.

'No, I'm not, as a matter of fact. I told you. I'm just going to be on my own. I'm very lucky to have been lent this room for two or three weeks while Ian's away.' Ian was her mother's brother and Jane felt he should be 'Uncle' Ian to her but he never was, it was all wrong, like everything else.

'You'll see – we'll work things through,' and her mother tried a small smile.

Jane looked at the tired, white face with a mixture of pity and resentment. Why should *we* work things through? she thought. Why should *I* have to do anything – it's your mess, not mine. I just want to have an ordinary life, go to the same school for longer than one year, make some friends, have a loo that works . . .

'You can take some of your school work up with you – perhaps Billa will go over some of your maths.'

'Huh, I can just imagine *that*,' Jane said sarcastically.

'You won't miss much school – it's half term for a week

anyway and Mrs Preston will give you some books. I've explained the situation to her, she's very understanding.'

So everybody knows all about our affairs at school now. That's brilliant! Jane rushed into the bedroom she shared with her mother and slammed the door.

The room was freezing cold. The draught from the ill-fitting window blew the skimpy blue curtain and let in the sound of dogs barking below. Wrapping a blanket round herself like a shawl, Jane sat huddled in a chair and thought about her sister. The seven year age gap made a big difference – they had nothing in common. Billa had been clever at school and, despite the disruptions, had done well in exams. She'd missed Dad when he'd gone and had buried herself in her books. There'd also been some rows, arguing, door banging. She won't want me; she's busy with her own life. From the rare, scrappy postcards she had sent, Jane gathered that Billa's digs at The Laurels were even more uncomfortable and cheerless than the Parkfield flat, if that was possible, but Billa had been full of it: 'Really lucky . . . probably due for demolition . . . bit like a squat . . . lots of us sharing . . . really great . . . !'

She heard the door of the flat close and a few moments later saw her mother going out to post a letter; from the third floor window she looked small and vulnerable as if she might be blown away in the wind. Jane went to put the kettle on for a pot of tea.

There was some geography homework she should be doing but someone in the next flat had turned up the volume on a jazz tape and somewhere a baby was screaming. I know just how it feels, she thought.

'I wish we could move from here, Mum,' she said later over

tea. In her mind's eye, she saw a neat little house with a lawn in a quiet road somewhere far away.

'I think we may have to – I don't think we can go on here much longer. I'm going to see a bedsit with shared bathroom down by the . . ' but Jane had switched off, she put her hands over her ears and started humming a tune.

The coach ride up to Liverpool seemed endless. No one spoke to her and she and her bulging plastic bags were jammed up against a fat woman who seemed to ooze over on to her seat. A man behind kept coughing and the air became stuffy. As the fat woman had the window seat, Jane couldn't see much of the passing view; it grew dark early anyway. She chewed at a cheese sandwich and hoped that Billa wouldn't forget to meet her at the bus station. She felt homesick already, even Parkfield Tower with their few belongings scattered untidily around was better than nowhere and she wondered what her mother was doing. The coach was slowing down and people were reaching for their luggage.

'Do you mind!' the fat woman said as Jane reached across her to peer out of the window. She gathered up her bags and jostled her way to the door of the coach and down the steep steps. Everyone, except her, either walked away briskly or was greeted and whisked off by friends or relatives. Jane looked round in panic – Billa hadn't come. She was here in a strange city all alone.

Suddenly she felt her long hair being tugged at the back and she swung round to see a friendly dark face peering down at her.

'Jane Sullivan from Watford?' He was about twenty and

had a nice jokey voice. She nodded and he bowed with mock courtesy. 'Shannon Shuntela from Zimbabwe, at your service. I bear greetings from one Billa who regrets she had a previous engagement – an audition with the Drama Society – and asked me to escort you to the Victorian extravaganza that is The Laurels.'

'You mean Billa sent you to meet me?' Jane asked with relief.

'Precisely.'

He picked up two of her plastic bags and led the way out into the cold October evening.

'D'you know Liverpool?'

'No . . . only The Beatles music,' Jane said.

'Yeah, yeah, yeah,' Shannon sang. 'It's a great city – wonderful buildings. Down there,' he waved one of the bags vaguely into the darkness, 'is The Pier Head, Liver Building, The Docks . . . but we're going this way, to catch the bus. There's St George's Hall . . . There's the Uni . . .' she had to run to keep up with his long strides, '. . . and this is the Adelphi Hotel – I'll point out the two cathedrals on our way. You must get Billa to show you round a bit while you're here.' Some hope of that, Jane thought. She couldn't imagine her sister bothering with a conducted tour for *her* benefit – she was always busy during the few days she spent at home, dashing here and rushing off there or getting a holiday job in the local cafe or shop. Jane realised she hardly knew her.

'And can you tell me,' Shannon was now asking, 'exactly why she is called Billa? Such an unusual name.'

Look who's talking, she thought, but said, 'She couldn't say "Elizabeth" properly when she was a baby.'

'Run!' he shouted suddenly. A bus was coming. They

reached the bus stop just in time. Shannon swung himself up, threw in the bags, and hauled Jane up; after collecting their tickets they collapsed into a couple of seats.

'I've . . . got . . . a . . . stitch,' Jane said, gasping for breath.

'Never mind that – look – the Anglican Cathedral,' Shannon rubbed at the steamed-up window.

She peered out at the rose-coloured, floodlit building.

'It's beautiful.'

A few seconds later he said 'Quick! Paddy's Wigwam!' and Jane caught a brief glimpse of a huge illuminated Christmas lantern before it was hidden.

'What is it?'

'The Roman Catholic Cathedral.' The commentary didn't stop even when the bus rattled along quieter streets, ill lit and lined with dingy, unkempt houses.

'And this is the . . .' His voice was soothing. Jane let it all wash over her. She closed her eyes – she felt as if she'd been travelling for days.

'Hey, wake up, here we are.' They were the only ones getting off the bus, which was nearly empty now. The pavement was slippery with wet leaves, more leaves were falling from overhanging trees and, by the light of passing cars, Jane could see monstrous houses set back from the road. Opposite were low railings, more trees and grass, like a park. Only one street lamp, further down, seemed to be working.

'Welcome to Garibaldi Gardens, former residences of Liverpool's crème de la crème – all very special in their own way – every one different – now sadly a shadow of their former glory.'

Jane wasn't sure what Shannon was rambling on about. A cold wind had got up and she was longing to sit still in the warmth, and with some food. She followed Shannon as he turned into a gateway minus its gates. Overgrown laurel bushes and other neglected shrubs straggled along a short drive leading to a front porch at the top of a flight of steps.

'The Laurels,' Shannon announced, almost proudly, Jane thought.

As if on cue, the moon suddenly came out from behind clouds and the massive bulk of the grotesque house appeared silhouetted before them – crouched threateningly, as if ready to spring: it reminded her of one she'd seen in a horror film.

'Well, what d'you think?'

She tried to think of a suitable word which wouldn't offend. 'It's very . . . grand.'

He seemed satisfied with this. 'Yes, it *is* grand. Grand people used to live here once.'

A dim light in the porch guided them up the leaf strewn and weedy path. Shannon took the uneven stone steps two at a time. 'We'll see if Billa's back.' The brown paint on the massive front door was peeling off in flakes; the small Yale lock seemed all wrong. Jane had expected a large impressive brass key to unlock such an important-looking door.

An inner hall led through an arch into a much larger one and Jane's heart sank. The icy air smelling of stale food and something worse struck with a sour blast: it had been warmer outside.

No rugs softened the chipped tiled floor, laid out in a geometric and garish pattern of dusty blues, reds, browns and something that might once have been cream. From the lofty ceiling hung a single unshaded light bulb which threw alarming shadows up the solid staircase on which had been left a pile of someone's dirty washing, some beer cans and a large packet of toilets rolls. It was hard to tell what colour the walls were. Festoons of cobwebs hung down and swayed gently.

None of this seemed to depress Shannon, though, and he whistled as he knocked loudly on a door on the left. Footsteps could be heard echoing, clattering down from the top of the stairs. Someone laughed; rock music, very loud, wafted down then a door slammed and all was silent again.

'No luck I'm afraid,' Shannon said, shrugging his shoulders. 'She shouldn't be long. She's lucky; she's got the dining room,' he indicated the closed door with his head, 'all to herself. Helen and Jo have "the drawing room". Kelly and Mike are in the old "morning room" and I share what I call "the garden flat", but it's really the old kitchen, with Pete and Ben. Judy has the larder. I've lost track of upstairs – about a dozen I think – they come and go.'

Three people came hurrying into the hall from outside – jostling, shoving, shouting loudly – and chased each other up the stairs, sending the empty beer cans flying. The cobwebs danced more vigorously in the sudden draught from the door.

'Look, you'd better come downstairs and I'll whiz up one of my magic meals. I'm famous for them – conjured up out of nothing!' Jane had plonked herself down on one of her plastic bags feeling as desolate and forlorn as the old house. She got up and followed him, too miserable to speak.

'This is what we call the guest room – for overflow of friends after a party,' he was nodding at a large inglenook fireplace with a carved inscription 'Improve the shining hour' at the other end of the hall. Jane could just make out a couple of mattresses topped by a stack of old newspapers with a black cat sitting on top.

'Now how did *she* get back in? Still she keeps down the mice population, I suppose.' He led the way through a door covered in some soft, green cloth, now tattered, and down steep wooden stairs into a cavernous room with frosted glass at the windows. A disused black cooking range was almost hidden by tottering piles of books. At a table surrounded by more books and a pile of dirty dishes, someone was busy writing – he looked up briefly and didn't look pleased at being disturbed.

'Jane – Pete. Pete – Jane,' Shannon made the introductions. 'Just going to whistle up one of my concoctions – "eggs erroneous", I think – if we've got any eggs.'

'There's work going on here in case you hadn't noticed,' Pete said.

'Please don't bother, I'm not hungry really.' Jane had caught sight of the large sink full of yet more dishes and some filthy pans, one of which Shannon had just picked up and was inspecting. 'Is this burnt porridge or what?' he asked Pete, who ignored the question. 'It's no bother, we've all got to eat,' and he busied himself with eggs, onions, baked beans, curry powder, sardines and a packet of cornflakes.

Jane turned away and pretended to be interested in some framed prints of buildings dotted around the walls. She tried to concentrate hard on some plans laid out on another table as she felt she was going to be sick any minute. There was a pungent smell rising from the pan.

'Look in the corner; we've got something rather special,' Shannon shouted across the room to her, 'a dumb waiter.'

Jane turned, startled, not knowing what to expect but didn't see anything very unusual. 'What's that?' she asked.

'It's a small . . .' but he didn't get any further as the door was suddenly pushed open and Billa stood there in long black skirt, baggy mustard sweater, a bulging canvas bag over one shoulder and her long blonde plait over the other.

'Hi,' she said and collapsed sprawling into a chair. 'Did Shannon meet you OK?' she asked Jane, who nodded. 'Thanks, you're a pal. What's that disgusting smell?'

Shannon ignored this but said, 'Did you get the part?'

'No such luck. Nick got it and she'll be hopeless. I'm a maid . . . Martha . . . Any chance of a coffee?'

Pete looked up briefly from his work and groaned.

'Sorry, sorry . . . We can take a hint, can't we?' Billa said to Jane, 'Come on, let's go. I picked up some fish and chips – we can have a feast.'

Jane thanked Shannon.

'My pleasure,' he said. 'We'll be seeing you around, I expect,' and returned to stirring his pan. Pete went on writing.

Billa unlocked the door to her room and switched on the light.

'Fling your bags down anywhere,' she said. 'Sorry about the mess – never have any time for clearing up. You can sleep over there.' She indicated a mattress on the floor in the bay window and then, sweeping a pile of books and take-away cartons to one side of a table, plonked down two paper parcels of fish and chips. 'You can organise the food tomorrow – it'll give you something to do.'

'Mum sends her love,' Jane said, trying to find a space somewhere to put her bags.

'I hope she gets this job – she deserves a break,' said Billa as she bent down and put a match to a small gas fire, which had been fitted into the black marble fireplace. 'By the way, gas is *very* expensive –so no using it in the daytime.' Warming her hands in the hissing pinkie-blue flame, Jane thought Billa sounded as if she was talking about a casual friend, rather than their mother. She glanced round the room, not able to take in all the chaos at once. Part of the faded wallpaper hung in strips. An upper pane of the window had been boarded over with plywood. Clothes were draped over a broken cane chair – a wardrobe in the corner had no door. Something that might have been ketchup stuck to the wall in a squiggle that looked like a question mark.

Billa had put some music on a small CD player and was laying out the fish and chips as if they were some delicacy. 'Right – come and get it,' she shouted.

'Put the kettle on for some coffee and I'll have mine black – got some reading to catch up on tonight – the water's in the cloakroom across the hall,' Billa said after they had eaten.

Jane was glad to find there was a loo in the cloakroom but it looked as if no amount of scrubbing or bleach would ever clear the dark stains: it looked as if toads might live down there.

'I'm really lucky to have this room. You should just see what *some* people have to put up with.' Billa kicked off her shoes and toasted her feet by the fire. 'The house is horrible – imagine just one family living in it – and there are heaps like it dotted round the park, like dinosaurs, relics of a bygone age! Of course, Shannon thinks they're terrific but then he's doing architecture and sees things differently.'

'The place looks as if it's falling down.'

'Well, that's the landlord's worry,' Billa said briskly, 'and talking of which – did Mum manage to scrape together last month's rent? What's the latest on the money situation?'

'I don't know – I think it's all right,' Jane lied. She felt uncomfortable discussing things like this. She knew exactly to the very pound what they had, what they needed. Her mother kept nothing back.

'And what about that letter Dad wrote,' Billa went on relentlessly, 'I thought she was getting some advice from that new solicitor.'

'I don't want to talk about it. I hate talking about it.' Jane banged down her mug of coffee, spilling a little on some papers lying nearby.

'Just look what you've done. My dissertation!' Billa screamed and dabbed at it with a tissue. 'And that's just typical of you, isn't it? Not wanting to talk about things, never facing up to anything – someone has to. You're just a little ostrich burying your head in the sand all the time. Well, you'd better go and bury your head in a cushion now – I've got work to do.' Billa curled her legs up on a battered sofa. Here, you'd better have these.' She chucked a blanket and a lumpy, stained cushion at Jane.

Feeling that she was being over fussy by bothering to undress in such surroundings, Jane lay down on the mattress in the bay window. She pulled the blanket over her and cried into the cushion, which smelt of cats.

Chapter 2

The alarm clock went off at seven and, for a minute, Jane wondered where she was. Even when the light was switched on she couldn't remember – the colourful Indian cotton bedspreads draped over the windows were unrecognisable, the bed felt strange – then it all came back.

Billa seemed in a better mood this morning, the music began again and she sang with it as she switched on the kettle. She searched around for a couple of bowls and put a packet of cornflakes on the table.

'I made up some powdered milk yesterday, it's in the fridge.'

Jane discovered the small fridge under a grubby towel. The door was a bit shaky and had been mended at some time with a large nail. Inside, a mug of very elderly baked beans, a bowl of something which had sprouted fur, and the jug of milk were the only occupants.

'Bread's in a tin somewhere if you can find it. I never bother much with breakfast; I have a bite at the college refectory for lunch. There may be some tins on a shelf in the cupboard,' Billa said uncertainly. 'You can always pop round to the shop on the corner of Croxton Park if we've run out.' She looked through some notes while she drank her coffee.

'Will you be gone all day?' Jane asked in a small voice, hardly audible over the rock music.

''Fraid so – lectures this morning and tutorial this afternoon, plus a meeting of the film society. Should be back about six. I'll give you the key – *don't lose it.* I'm off to join the queue for the cloakroom.'

Jane kept her fingers wrapped round her coffee mug for warmth, wondering how to fill in the hours that lay ahead. When Billa returned, she gathered up a pile of books and papers then, glancing in an ornate, discoloured mirror over the mantelpiece, started to plait her hair. She caught sight of her sister's reflection, drooping over the table, and felt irritated. 'Don't wander off and get lost or anything like that – I suppose while you're here I've got to be responsible for you, although—' she broke off but Jane could imagine the next . . . I didn't ask to have you here, I don't want you here, you're nothing but a nuisance . . .

'What can I do all day?' Jane asked. Billa turned round and gave her a long hard stare.

'What d'you mean, what can you do all day? Who d'you think I am – your entertainment manager? You can get on with some of your school work for a start.'

'It's so cold in here and there's no room to put anything . . .' Jane began.

'You're pathetic, aren't you! Grow up! What are you next birthday? You need to get yourself organised, be a proper paid-up member of the family.'

'You sound like some old headteacher,' Jane shouted. 'You live in a horrible hole like this and you tell me to get organised!' And what family? she thought – we don't have a proper family: a grandmother they never saw, who lived in the north of Scotland, Uncle Ian, always on the move, and somewhere other grandparents who she couldn't remember.

'Horrible hole, is it? Well, you know what you can do, don't you?' Billa looked as if she was about to explode, then, looking at her watch, she yelled, 'I'm going to miss the bus! Look,' she seemed to relent a bit, 'if I can finish this essay tonight, I might skip a lecture tomorrow and we could go out somewhere but don't bank on it.' She managed a half smile and snatched up a shapeless old tweed jacket, opened the door, slammed it behind her and was gone.

I suppose I could try and tidy up a bit, Jane thought, but then abandoned the idea. She wouldn't know where to start and she'd probably put things in all the wrong places and make Billa even more mad. But I can rinse the mugs and bowls. Carrying them to the cloakroom she nearly crashed into Shannon, who was rushing by, swinging a large roll of drawings. 'Washing up?' he asked. 'That'll make a change. Got a busy day planned?'

'Not really but I'm meant to get something ready for supper – there's no food in.'

'Worry not! If all else fails, you can come and have a Shuntela special . . . Chilli Con Everything – that's on the menu tonight.'

The smell of last night's meal still lingered in the hall. 'Thanks,' Jane said, making a mental note to buy some eggs for a simple omelette.

'And if you find you've got a minute to spare, do me a favour. I've been meaning to talk to Billa about it but keep forgetting. The dumb waiter . . . Should appear in the old dining room . . . Look out for it. Oh and,' he paused before going out of the front door, 'Helen and Jo have a TV set. They bought it at a car boot sale. You have to bang it on the side from time to time . . . very temperamental – but it *sometimes* works – just in case you get desperate. I'll be seeing you.'

'Thanks,' Jane said again automatically but she hadn't really taken in the last bit. A dumb waiter – he'd mentioned it last night. The place must be haunted.

When she returned to the room, she looked round nervously, half expecting to see an apparition – a silent footman in old-fashioned clothes with staring eyes, beckoning to her. She couldn't stay here all day. She'd have to go out – buy some eggs at the shop Billa had mentioned.

She turned off the music. The silence made things even worse and gave her a feeling of isolation. Grabbing her anorak she hurried out, but being outside wasn't much better. Everyone else seemed to be rushing round with a purpose and she looked with envy at groups of chattering children going to school accompanied by parents or friends; people hurrying to work or college, all busy, taken up with their own affairs; even dogs going for walks had a sense of purpose about them. It was only just starting to get light – a pale sun filtered through the autumn leaves, but it was still very cold. The park opposite seemed to stretch away for miles, with grassy banks and clumps of beech and oak trees, reminding Jane of the real country she'd seen on an outing once to a stately home. Only the muffled roar of morning traffic gave away the fact that this was just a city park.

She could see the old houses dotted around the crescent more clearly now. Each one was different – some yellow brick, others red, some had a turret or a balcony or an impressive porch, with fancy brickwork – but they had one thing in common, she thought, they were all hideous.

One had become an Indian restaurant, the Kathmandu, Jane noticed as she dawdled along. Another was now a dentist's surgery. The Hollies had become a hotel offering bargain-price buffet lunches and some looked as run down as The Laurels, with crumbling gate pillars and drainpipes clinging on at crazy angles and overgrown spruce, birch and holly trees threatening to strangle the lot in a prickly green grip.

A jogger ran by with a resolute look in her eye and made Jane feel she should quicken up her own pace. A side street led to the busy main road and on the corner she found a small General Stores. Inside it was warm; she was the only customer.

'Half a dozen eggs please and . . .' Jane decided to spin out her shopping for as long as she could.

The woman behind the counter was friendly. 'No school today?'

'I don't really live round here, I'm staying with my sister at The Laurels,' Jane said, inspecting a tin of pilchards.

'That's next door but one to The Oaks, isn't it? My grandfather was gardener there in the twenties. Of course they've all changed hands a lot since then – wonderful old houses in their heyday. But they've come down in the world now.'

'Mmm,' Jane agreed. 'How much are those?' she pointed to some filled batch cakes, wondering if she could afford one for her lunch.

'Ninety-five pence. Of course, they go back a long way before the twenties. Victorian they are. Cotton and shipping families mostly. Lots of money. Some of those houses have ballrooms and even in my grandfather's day he used to have to mark out the tennis court and set up the croquet hoops. He'd turn in his grave if he could see the state of The Oaks now – been turned into a Social Club or something.'

'Mmm . . . sad,' Jane said, fingering a grapefruit. She wasn't really very interested in the fate of old houses. Someone came into the shop and she had to make up her mind quickly.

'Two apples, six eggs, a tin of sardines and four tomatoes, please.'

Finding a bench in the park, she took an apple out of the bag and started nibbling at it. The sun had gone in and it was turning colder; as she swallowed the bits of apple they seemed to chill her stomach. She started to shiver and encouraged a spaniel to come and sit near her for warmth but as rain started to fall steadily, the dog leapt off the seat and ran away.

Jane gazed after him and then looked back towards The Laurels, standing grim and desolate. I suppose there's nothing else for it, she thought, feeling depressed. I'll have to go back there and wait for Billa.

The trees were dripping now as she turned in at the gate and her pale anorak was turning a blotchy navy. She unlocked the front door with one of the keys; wet footprints appeared on the dusty tiles as she walked across the hall. No one seemed to be about and it was so dark she could hardly see the keyhole to Billa's door. She could hear the rain fall slanting against the huge stained-glass landing window.

Once in, she snapped on the light quickly, even the single naked bulb made the room look a little less gloomy. She switched on Billa's reading lamp on the table and picked up some of the work she was supposed to do. Her anorak dripped steadily where she'd hung it in the corner – she could hear the drips falling on to the cracked dinner plate underneath. It was hard to concentrate on the maths problems. They seemed silly, they didn't make sense, she read them over and over again. Why would a man want to fill a cylinder with oil just so that he could measure the quantity? She put the kettle on for a mug of coffee. There were sounds now from overhead, creaks and footsteps and she tried not to think of the lurking dumb waiter, who might be watching, waiting.

The poem she'd been told to learn by heart was no easier than the maths. The lines just ran round in her mind and then escaped, refusing to stay there.

When icicles hang by the wall
And Dick the Shepherd blows his nail
When Tom bears logs into the hall
And milk comes frozen home in pail . . .

She started to shiver again.

Frozen home in pail
Icicles hang by the . . .

Hanging in the doorless wardrobe, she caught sight of Billa's famous fake fur coat – the envy of her friends, which she'd bought at a bargain price at Oxfam. Slipping it on, Jane felt like an animal in a pantomime – all floppy paws – but it was snug and warm and she nestled down into it, rolling up one sleeve so that she could hold the mug. As she took a scalding sip, she heard a faint noise, something between a howl and a whine; it seemed to echo from the depths of the earth. Then it died away.

She tried to busy herself, flicking over pages of some of

Billa's books, reassuring herself that it was just the wind whistling round the house. She huddled further down into the fur coat; the books all looked boring. Then it started again – a thin wailing and it couldn't be the wind, the trees outside were sodden but still now.

There was a cupboard built up into the wall behind a rack of Billa's clothes – it seemed to be coming from there and yet underground.

I must lock it, then I'll be safe, she thought, and crept cold and frightened towards the cupboard, the coat dragging behind her. But it was a sliding oak door with no bolt or key, just a funny little carved knob. As she touched it with icy fingers, testing it to see if it was securely closed, it started to slide back. Horrified, she ducked down on all fours, her head covered by the coat, holding her breath, waiting for something to pounce out at her.

After a minute or two of stillness when nothing had happened, she forced herself to peep out. There was now a large gap in the wall, where the door had slid back. Inside the darkness nothing moved, there was no sound.

Just an empty old cupboard with a shelf, that's all, Jane thought – but I'm still going to seal it up and she looked round for some strong cord to tie onto the knob and loop round the tarnished brass light bracket.

All she could find was a pair of green tights – they'll have to do.

Curiosity compelled her to have a hasty look inside. There seemed to be nothing there except a thin, taut rope, stretched from top to bottom on the right hand side . . . but there was something else. Against the left side, hardly visible, she saw a small silver ball by a large black box, standing on end, which had at first appeared to be part of the cupboard. 'Go on – open it,' a voice seemed to tell her.

She climbed up awkwardly into the recess, forgetting how frightened she'd been. It was a tight squeeze. It's probably empty or full of boring old papers, she thought as she heaved the box over. But it couldn't be – even in the half light, silver crescent moons and golden suns shone out from the dark shiny lid, a crazy zigzag pattern framed the border, glowing flames licked round the initials 'A.J.P.'.

This was no ordinary box – it couldn't be empty, something special had to be hoarded in a box like this. Her fingers pulled impatiently at the delicate catch, then pushed back the lid very gently.

She couldn't believe it, it *was* empty. Disappointed, she touched the inside – glossy and smooth – but too shallow. Surely it should have been deeper. Suddenly she understood. A false bottom! To make it look empty! Squatting on her heels in the cramped space, she pulled up the top, lacquered tray and underneath saw a curious jumble of goodies. Taking them out carefully one by one, she set them out in colourful array around her. Soft silk scarves, tubes, blocks with numbers, silver rings, pieces of coloured string, candles, coloured balls, coins, discs, fans, flags, masks, handkerchiefs, a black velvet pouch.

She stared down, then lifted up a black, pointed hat studded with stars and spangles, which had been lying folded away at the bottom. A magician's hat! Tracing the curves of a shooting star, she remembered, with a shiver of excitement, a party long ago when a man, small, bald and with a speedy patter, had wound up his conjuring act with an announcement – 'And now, I shall make you *disappear*!' Her friend, Lorna, had stepped into a chest and, with a wave of his wand, had vanished. And here was a similar wand in this box of magic tricks.

Everything had been carefully packed away. Then suddenly spotting again the shining silver ball – the size of an egg – she cupped it. As she pressed a tiny switch at the top, it flew open to reveal a watch – but it wasn't *just* a watch, it also played a faint tune. Jane couldn't recognise the music; it might have been a nursery rhyme. When it had repeated the theme twice, it stopped. There was something engraved in flowery decorative writing and she had to hold it very close to decipher the words.

'Backward, turn backward,
O Time, in your flight . . .'

There was a little more but it was difficult to read. The watch had stopped at five to three. She shook it gently and tried to wind the switch to re-start it but, with a whirring sound and a will of its own, the fingers started to turn backwards, faster and faster. She grew dizzy, mesmerised looking at them – round and round as if they would never stop. Swaying on her heels, she reached out to steady herself and, feeling the rigid hard rope at the side, clung on to it for support.

As she pulled, the light seemed to vanish altogether and with sick horror, Jane felt herself falling down and down, whirling, spinning, plunging like a rider on the terrifying 'loop the loop' at the fairground. Then, with a sickening jolt, the plummeting stopped. She couldn't breathe properly, she couldn't see and her bones felt jangled and jarred. Worst of all, she suddenly knew she was going to be sick any minute all over Billa's precious coat.

I must get out of here, she thought with panic, I've got to get out. She pressed the sides of the cupboard, desperately trying to work out the position of the sliding door, but she'd lost her bearings. I might be imprisoned for ever.

Pushing hard at the third side, she felt it budge slightly and, with another heave, the door slid away abruptly and she fell out onto a floor, hard as a pavement.

Something was terribly wrong. This wasn't Billa's room. Instead of cold and chaos, here was cleanliness and order and a wonderful smell, which seemed to wrap the whole room in a warm blanket. Bread, baking – she'd loved the smell as a small child at her grandmother's in Scotland – it spelt cosiness, security.

A wall clock ticked and something in a large black pan bubbled away, rattling the lid.

There was something about the room that was vaguely familiar. The frosted glass and the black shiny cooking range. She was in a kitchen – but whose? And how had she arrived here? She looked back at the hole in the wall, trying to work it out. It looked like a small lift but if she'd come straight down she'd be in Shannon's room and this room was nothing like that . . . Except the windows and the . . .

Someone was coming: slow, padding footsteps drew near then stopped. There was a piercing scream.

'Ooooooo! Whatever is it?'

Looking up, Jane saw a puzzled face and a pair of capable floury hands waving over her in agitation.

'What am I doing here? I should be upstairs,' Jane asked. 'Where am I?'

'Good gracious – it speaks! Thought you were a great furry animal crouched on my kitchen floor.'

The face wasn't unkind, Jane saw. It was topped by hair the colour of salt and pepper with a white cap perched on top. Then the bewilderment and doubt suddenly vanished and she smiled. 'Of course, you must be Grace. You're Miss Muriel's daughter (or Mrs Devine, as she now is). Remember your mother when she was just your age. She was a funny little thing too. You must have come in the back door. You're quite right, you *should* be upstairs – they'll be expecting you. Ivy! She shouted loudly and at the same time pulled Jane to her feet. 'I don't know what's come over that girl lately. Never there when needed and looks white as a ghost. Sickening for something if you ask me,' she confided in Jane, who didn't know how to reply.

Ivy didn't appear.

'I'm Mrs Murphy.' She looked critically at Jane. 'You're not really very like your mother – take after your father, I dare say, not that I've ever seen *him* . . . Come along with me. I'll show you the way. Hurry up now – I've got to get back to my pastry.'

Up the stone stairs – hadn't she come down them yesterday evening with Shannon? Why was she here now with this plump woman, now complaining about her varicose veins, and wearing long old-fashioned looking clothes and a huge white apron. Why was someone expecting her?

Through the door, covered in the same green material but not in tatters any more, then Mrs Murphy said, 'My poor legs – they're like boiled beetroots. Off you go now – Miss Lucy will still be at her lessons but there'll be somebody in the morning room.' She indicated the first door on the right then plodded off down the stairs calling, 'Ivy! Ivy!'

The green door swung to. Jane was left alone and there was

Billa's room, second on the right and surprisingly the door was wide open. She looked round the door expecting to see the now familiar hodge podge . . . but stood transfixed. It was the same room certainly – she was sure it was, windows, fireplace, even the ornate mirror were there in their place but everything else had vanished – this was a dining room, gleaming, spotless. The large mahogany table reflected silver candelabras and arrangements of orange and white chrysanthemums. Heavy velvet curtains caught up with tassels hung at the windows and, against dark green wallpaper, hung portraits in gilded frames. It was a rich room, a beautiful room, Jane thought, but where were all Billa's bits and pieces?

'Bazooka!'

She swung round, startled at the sound of a soft, deep voice behind her. A mountain of a man with whiskery face and big smile was waving a plump hand as if he'd conjured her out of the air.

'Dolly, jolly, zambo!'

She couldn't understand any of this.

'Hey presto – magicked out of the air!' He looked pleased and she was relieved that she could recognise a few words.

'From whence did you spring? In his plush, dark velvet jacket, he resembled a well-fed, contented mole. About him hung a smoky smell that wasn't cigarettes but something altogether stronger, more aromatic.

'I've really come from *that* room,' she pointed to Billa's, 'but suddenly found myself downstairs and now I'm *here*.'

He clapped his hands in delight. 'Splendid. It *is* a magic trick. Now, I'll tell you what really happened. You went to the back door by mistake – though why poor Muriel let you come into the house by yourself, goodness only knows. Then you came up from the kitchen, had a look in the dining room and . . . here you are. And you're Grace and I'm your Uncle Dolly and we've been waiting for you. Come along into the morning room and I'll go and inform my mother and the others that you've arrived.'

There was no way of arguing with him, he just led the way towards the room opposite Billa's and she noticed now that the hall floor was gleaming. Two or three red Turkish rugs were scattered around, a tall grandfather clock stood against one wall and in the inglenook fireplace, which Shannon had described as the 'guest room', a real fire burned – crackling with sticks and logs.

She began to say, 'I think I'm in the wrong house,' but just then the clock chimed, the echo from the loud deep bell reverberating round the lofty hall and she couldn't even hear her own voice.

The morning room was a dark, cosy cave with firelight sending up glowing reflections on the highly polished furniture. Outside it was still raining but here all was warmth and comfort. A daily newspaper lay on a leather chair and the air had the same pleasing, smoky smell as Uncle Dolly. He was just as an uncle should be – his name was funny but he was sunny and friendly.

'Now, you wait here,' he said, 'and by the way – what a *very* fashionable coat.' He gave a soft laugh; she didn't know if he was teasing and she didn't mind. He disappeared, then a second later popped his head round the door again and, beaming, said, 'Plum duff for luncheon today!'

Jane felt at home and welcome. They'd obviously been expecting someone called Grace and she'd turned up. It might be nice to go on being Grace just a little while longer before the explanations began and she must trail out into the rain again and see what had happened to The Laurels.

Left on her own, she glanced idly around – what a lot of furniture for one room. A cigar butt lay smouldering in a heavy glass ash tray by the newspaper on the arm of the chair. An oak roll-top desk looked weighed down by sepia photographs in silver and wooden frames. A tortoiseshell calendar gave the date. She looked again . . . it was all wrong . . . it said 1892. The day and the month were all right but someone had fiddled with the year. She'd better not touch it, someone might come.

Looking round the door into the hall to see if Uncle Dolly was on his way back, she saw something which shocked her. Over the mantelpiece in the inglenook was the carved text she'd noticed last night: 'Improve the shining hour'. Shannon's words came back to her. 'All these houses are different . . . each one is unique. No two alike.' *Was* it The Laurels? How could it be? Frantically she grabbed the newspaper. It looked different, the print was strangely thick and black, the photographs all old fashioned. She looked at the date – it was the same as the calendar, 1892.

Chapter 3

Footsteps were approaching and there stood Uncle Dolly again. Gently he took the newspaper away from Jane. 'Full of nasty stories. Come along now. Mother is waiting.' No time to say anything – and how could she even begin to explain when even *she* didn't know what had happened?

Across the hall again and this time Uncle Dolly opened a door on the left.

'So this is poor Muriel's girl.' An elderly woman with white hair and black lace cap sat in a high-backed chair. Her feet rested on a footstool in front of a fire so that Jane had the impression she was in the presence of royalty seated on a throne.

'Come a little nearer.'

Jane obeyed and her foot caught in the hem of Billa's coat. Uncle Dolly saved her from sprawling, 'Whoops a daisy.'

'Good gracious, child, what on earth is that you're wearing? And your hair . . . so straight. I always knew poor Cousin Muriel had a bohemian streak . . . never mind, we won't go into all that now. I am your Great Aunt but you may call me "Grandma" while you are here, like Lucy and Henry. And this is your Aunt Lallie and your Aunt Flora – your mother's cousins.' Two women in sweeping dresses materialised from the shadows and flanked Grandma.

'Grace, you may kiss me.' Jane was given a little push by Uncle Dolly. Grandma was smiling graciously. Aunt Lallie was holding her arms out and Aunt Flora's eyes were moist and sentimental. Jane had never felt so welcome anywhere. She heard herself saying, as if from a long way off, 'I'm called Jane. Jane's my second name.' She kissed the dry, white face – the wrinkled skin reminded her of crepe paper – then let herself be hugged and overpowered by lavender by the two aunts.

'You don't say Grace, eh?' Uncle Dolly rumbled with laughter at his little joke. 'Don't say Grace.'

'Very well, *Jane* it shall be. How is your mother?' Grandma asked.

'She's . . . all right.' Jane felt it would be safe to say this.

'And – your father?'

'I'm not sure.'

'What do you mean "not sure"?'

This was a bit more tricky. 'I haven't seen him much lately,' she tried to keep it vague.

'How typical. I suppose he shuts himself up in his studio all the time. That's an artist for you – well, I warned Muriel, didn't I?'

'You did, Mother,' Uncle Dolly said.

'And she just sent the child round on her own.' Grandma shook her head. 'And hasn't got two pennies to rub together by the looks of it.' She eyed Jane critically. 'Never mind. I know my duty. Family is family. Where would we be without it?'

It was like a small speech and without thinking Jane said, 'I quite agree. The trouble is—'

Grandma raised an eyebrow. 'I don't remember asking for any opinion,' she said evenly, 'children should be kept in their place.'

Jane nearly said, 'hear, hear.' It was like a great weight being lifted from her mind. Someone who understood that she *wanted* to be kept in her place: she didn't *want* to be treated as if she was thirty instead of a twelve year old, with big decisions to make, shared confidences about money and health, where they should live, do their shopping . . .

'Lucy should be finishing her lessons in five minutes.' Grandma consulted a watch pinned like a brooch on her stiff black dress. 'After luncheon you may go for a walk in the park if the rain stops. *We*,' she turned to one of her daughters, 'are going to Aigburth Crescent to visit Mrs Grenville.'

'Mother,' Aunt Lallie said softly, 'couldn't Flora go in my place? I have so many letters to write.'

'Mrs Grenville particularly wished to see you, Lallie. I think she may ask you to join her hospital committee – it would be a great privilege!'

A gong was struck out in the hall. Starting with a melodious boom, boom, boom, it grew louder and ended with a triumphant volley, dying away on an echo.

'Plum duff!' Uncle Dolly said excitedly.

Into the room dashed a slender girl of about Jane's age, her looks so delicate, Jane thought she might shatter into a thousand fragments if she fell; her dark curls flopped over a full, bottle-green dress. She stopped short when she saw Jane, and stared.

'Walk, girl, don't run like that,' Grandma said. 'This is Cousin Muriel's girl, Grace – who prefers to be called Jane for some reason. Don't stare, it's very rude, Lucy. Now, say "hello" to Jane and take her into luncheon.'

Lucy was staring at the coat in amazement.

'You must take off that . . . abomination,' Grandma nodded at Jane. 'Hide it away somewhere until it's time for her to return home,' she said to Uncle Dolly, who helped to slip the coat off Jane's shoulders. She was wearing jeans and a sweat shirt underneath. Grandma drew in her breath sharply. The two aunts gasped and Lucy put her hand over her mouth to hide a grin.

'To think,' Grandma said, 'that Muriel has sunk to this! She may wear one of your pinafores over . . .' She sought words to describe the jeans but failed. 'Quickly now.'

Seated round a smaller table in the bay window of the dining room, Jane looked round and approved of what she saw. The muddle and confusion previously reflected in the large mirror over Billa's mantelpiece was now replaced by harmony. The six sat talking pleasantly, eating small mouthfuls of mutton, potatoes and cauliflower with gravy and redcurrant jelly. Ivy, pale and sullen with dark nervous eyes, passed quietly among them, placing dishes and tureens down carefully. The white starched pinafore Jane now wore smelt clean, like fresh air.

A gas fire in exactly the same place as Billa's was fully lit. Outside the rain fell on to a neat front garden with trimmed hedges and tidy shrubs. A horse and carriage was going past in the road. The talk was of the weather, the afternoon's excursion – gentle, restful topics and Jane felt comfortable. 1892 was a good year to live in, she'd be quite happy to stay here – for a while, anyway. She hated the idea of the real Grace turning up to disrupt everything.

'Grandma says we might go to Southport one day for an expedition on the train some time. Would you like that?' Lucy was asking her.

'Sounds brilliant.'

Lucy looked at her in a strange way but said nothing.

There was a curious sound coming from the corner by the door and twisting round, Jane saw Ivy standing by the very cupboard into which she had crawled when she had opened up the black box. The door was slid back and she watched in frightened fascination to see what would be revealed this time.

'Have you never seen a dumb waiter before, Jane? Now turn round and sit up straight. I've never seen anyone slouch so much,' Grandma said.

A dumb waiter. That's what Shannon had been talking about. It must be used to send food and dishes up from the kitchen. Jane was very ready to turn round. She didn't want to look at the dumb waiter at all, feeling that somehow it might magic her back again to her other life. She stared hard at the crisp white frill round the arm of the pinafore and willed herself to stay.

Uncle Dolly startled her by clapping his hands. 'Here it is!' He smiled as Ivy carried to the table a round, honey-coloured crusty pudding. It oozed plums and juice when he cut into it.

'Mrs Murphy makes a wonderful duff.'

'Remind me to take a jar of her preserved plums to poor Miss Entwistle this afternoon. And I must leave one of my cards for the new people at The Elms.'

'Is Mr Povey-Reeves very rich, Grandma?' Lucy asked through a mouthful of pudding.

'Don't speak with your mouth full . . . and, as your Grandfather used to say, it is vulgar to talk of money. Mr

Povey-Reeves, like us, has a certain position to keep up. He's in sugar and spices,' she said by way of explanation to her daughters, 'and has a son in the Army, I believe.'

While being handed the jug of egg custard to swamp her plum duff, Jane glanced up at Aunt Flora, whose faded features had turned quite pink – the watery blue eyes looked agitated for a moment. A drop of custard hung off the bottom of the blue china jug and dropped on to the polished table. Flora dabbed at it with her napkin but Grandma hadn't noticed – she was savouring her food, sticky and sweet. 'Your father's favourite pudding,' she said and glanced fondly at the portrait of a gimlet-eyed gentleman over the mantelpiece.

Lucy scraped back her chair. 'Please may I leave the table?'

'You've bolted your food again, haven't you?' Grandma said, 'but yes, you may get down now – go and show Jane where she is to sleep and find something suitable for her to wear. I expect Miss Norris will organise some embroidery or art if the rain persists.' They were being dismissed.

Jane rushed past the dumb waiter – it yawned open looking like a mouth ready to gobble her up. She stumbled against Lucy.

'Walk, don't run,' Lucy said, imitating Grandma, but then laughed. 'Shall I show you round first? I've been counting the minutes till you arrived. This is the morning room where Uncle Dolly smokes his cigars and reads the newspaper,' and she pushed open the door.

'I know, I've been in here. What's that room next to the lounge?'

'Lounge? You mean drawing room, don't you? It's the study. That's the way down to Mrs Murphy's kitchen,' she said, pointing to the green door.

'I know that too. I haven't been upstairs though. I thought Uncle Dolly was your father.' They started climbing up the stairs and Lucy looked back at her, laughing again. 'You don't know anything, do you? Uncle Dolly is father's brother; Aunt Lallie and Aunt Flora are his sisters. Grandma is their mother and Grandfather, who died before I was born, was their father. Your mother is one of my father's cousins so I suppose we're second cousins or first cousins once removed. Jessie is our parlour maid. Mrs Murphy – the cook, Ivy . . . well . . . Ivy's a maid of all work and Goff is our gardener and looks after the horse and carriage and there's the gardener's boy, Sam. Grandma took him on as "an act of charity" she said, and Henry is my brother – he's thirteen – I'm nearly twelve. He's at school, lucky, lucky thing. *I* have to suffer Miss Norris and so will you for a few days but not tomorrow, it's Saturday. I think that's everybody. Do you go to school? I'm not strong enough.' She was out of breath after all this but only for a moment.

'Grandfather Patterson designed this,' she waved a fragile hand towards the stained-glass window. 'It represents some of his collections – glass, silver, china, paintings and his motto "Beauty is truth, truth beauty". He was a . . . connoisseur,' she brought the word out slowly.

It looked like the window above a sacred altar; Jane studied the yellow and purple shapes of glass. They reflected on Lucy's sallow face, giving it an oriental appearance.

The landing was dark with plum-coloured walls.

'This is Grandma's bedroom,' Lucy indicated a door firmly shut, and these are Uncle Dolly's, Aunt Lallie's and Aunt Flora's; and bathroom. Now we go up to *our* floor.'

'Just a minute – what happens up there?' Jane had spied a smaller staircase leading up into darkness.

'The room up there is kept locked. Nobody is *ever* allowed to go into it.' Lucy didn't give any clues why, and raced lightly up to the second floor.

'My bedroom – and your bed is over there—' They looked briefly into a spacious room dominated by two white and brass bedsteads covered with multi-coloured patchwork quilts, then Lucy darted off again. 'Bathroom.' Then her voice sank to a whisper, 'the school room – it used to be our nursery: Miss Norris has her lunch there on a tray, and this is Henry's room but he doesn't get home from school until tea-time.' She pushed open the door. All was quiet but over by the window sitting motionless in the gloom, Jane saw the silhouette of a boy.

'Henry, what are you doing here – why are you home?' Lucy asked.

Henry turned round startled. He looked as if he was all dressed up for a special ceremony, Jane thought, with his knickerbockers, waistcoat, braided jacket and high-collared shirt. His dark hair accentuated the pallor of his face and the shadows under his eyes made him look as if he hadn't slept for a week.

He was silent for a minute, as if trying to think of an excuse, then explained that sport had been cancelled because of the weather

'I slipped in through the back door so as not to disturb Grandma – no need to tell her. And now, I'm sorry, I've got work to do,' he said, after shaking hands formally with Jane, 'Latin and Greek.'

'How can you see in the dark?' Jane asked but Henry looked far away, not listening . . . It seemed as if he was there but not there.

'Henry used to be fun,' Lucy said, sighing, when the door had closed behind them, 'but he has his head in his books all the time now. Exams. He has to pass them before he can enter the Senior School.'

'Tough,' Jane said, not taking much interest.

'You say things in a funny way – do artists speak like that?'

'Mmm, probably.'

'The maids and cook sleep on the next floor, you can't see the back stairs from our landing.' Lucy resumed her guiding, 'and now I suppose we'd better go and see Miss Norris.'

Jane felt there was something missing. 'What about your mother, where is she?'

'Oh,' Lucy turned to her, her face was now blank and expressionless. 'She was taken just after I was born – we never speak of her.'

Never speak of her! Did 'taken' mean 'dead'? For a second Jane imagined Mum and Billa, how they would have turned this scrap of information upside down, inside out, shaken it vigorously into tatters and dissected each piece. Much better, like Lucy and her family, to simply put it away out of mind.

'What about your father?'

'He died fighting in Afghanistan. He was in the Lancashire Fusiliers,' she said proudly. 'Henry has his medals. I never knew him. I'm an orphan. That's why Henry and I live here with Grandmother.'

Miss Norris sat in the grey and white school room. She was wearing a long dove-grey skirt with a white ruffled shirt and was rather grey and colourless herself. She put some small pieces of coal on the fire with brass tongs and suggested they go for a nature walk now that the rain was easing off.

Snug in a navy dress with puffed sleeves and sash belonging to Lucy and a borrowed coat with a large collar, Jane enjoyed a tranquil stroll round the footpaths of the park while Miss Norris, in a thin, reedy voice, delivered a few sparse facts about trees and birds.

After tea of boiled eggs, bread and butter and seed cake in the school room, Miss Norris went home to a small house 'a tram ride away', where she lived with her elderly father, and Lucy announced, 'A great treat tonight! Uncle Dolly is giving a rehearsal. There's going to be a big concert in the church hall soon to raise money to replace the church silver: it disappeared twenty years ago. The new Vicar says it should be a community effort so everyone is doing something to help.'

'How did it disappear? Do you mean it was stolen?' Jane asked.

'It just . . . vanished,' Lucy said. She glanced round for a moment as if she might be overheard. 'My friend, Sybil, who used to have lessons with me, said *everyone* knew what had happened but nothing could be proved. The man was terribly poor – ten children to feed and that's why Grandma said it was an act of charity to take Sam Wills, the youngest son, as gardener's boy – it was Aunt Flora's idea.'

The only sound to be heard as they crept quietly down to the drawing room was the low whistle from gas jets lighting the stairs. All was quiet behind closed bedroom doors.

In the drawing room Lucy patted a small sofa for Jane to sit beside her. Mysterious rustlings came from a mountain of greenery banked up in a conservatory which opened out of the far end of the room. Aunt Flora was now running her fingers up and down the keyboard of a grand piano, which was draped in a Kashmir shawl.

Jane gazed around – she'd never seen so many objects gathered together in one room, even Billa's, but unlike *her* oddments, these were carefully placed, well polished, treasured. China ornaments, bowls, vases, photographs, small display cabinets. Jostling for space on the mantelpiece were blue and white plates, matching jars, invitations, yet more photographs, an ornate clock and some small stuffed birds perched on a branch, under a glass dome.

Wall space was filled with paintings, oil and watercolour, samplers, mirrors, arrangements of fans and feathers and the richly patterned carpet could hardly be seen for button-back chairs, wing armchairs, footstools, small tables – which in turn were covered by embroidery, letters, books – and a large table with a velvet fringed cloth, where the remains of afternoon tea were now being cleared away by the parlour maid, Jessie.

'What does Uncle Dolly do? Sing?' Jane asked Lucy.

'Wait and see.'

Henry slipped in quietly and pulled up a footstool near the conservatory, which was on a higher level, so that it looked like a small stage.

Entering to an imaginary fanfare of trumpets, Grandma appeared, tapping at the floor with her heavy walking stick, as if to make sure it was solid. She made her way to her large, plush wing armchair and was fussed over by Aunt Lallie. Everyone rose and stood until, with a wave of her black-mittened hand, she gestured for everyone to be seated.

Everything was hushed apart from the comfortable noises of the fire and the ticking of the clocks.

There was an air of expectancy. Aunt Flora struck a few chords, then played a haunting little tune which sounded somehow familiar to Jane. Suddenly she jumped and clutched at Lucy's skinny arm. As they watched, there was an explosion of light, a massive figure in top hat and twirling black cloak materialised from behind a potted palm, waving an ivory wand.

'Bazooka!' he said in a huge voice and the wand amazingly changed into a bunch of crimson and yellow flowers. No sooner were these thrown to one side, than soft silk handkerchiefs in jewel colours appeared as if from nowhere – more and more. As soon as they materialised from his busy fingers, they were discarded, fluttering away.

'Dolly, jolly, zambo!'

Magic tricks; of course. The box I found and the watch with that music – they were Uncle Dolly's, thought Jane.

'One, two, *three*!' He had taken off his top hat and, dipping down deep inside, produced a wriggling white mouse, to the accompaniment of some strident chords on the piano.

Lucy clapped but Grandma said, 'Put that animal away, Dolly!' and the mouse was dropped out of sight behind a fern.

Coloured balls were then conjured up from behind his ears and a brown speckled egg from behind Jane's.

'And now, for my next trick, could I have somebody from the audience, please?'

'Go on, Henry,' Lucy said, prodding her brother, who was in a daydream. He stood up by Uncle Dolly and while they talked of this and that, without anyone realising, was robbed of all the contents of his pocket. His handkerchief, with which

Uncle Dolly mopped his brow, a pencil, an envelope and a comb. It was miraculous, there were cheers. Bewitching and exotic flowers unfurled slowly from tiny blue folds of paper, lit by a taper. Striped skittles were juggled high in the air and were joined by spotted discs until Jane thought they must all come crashing down. Dramatic chords, played with a flourish, shook the piano. The show was over.

'Isn't he clever?' Lucy said.

'Brilliant.'

The gong sounded in the hall. The show was over. Everyone clapped. 'Bravo.'

'I have two or three new tricks up my sleeve,' Uncle Dolly said, emerging from the jungle, 'but they need a bit of brushing up so I may ask for an assistant before my next rehearsal.'

'Come along, Adolphus. The gong has rung for dinner. Give me your arm.' Grandma said, beginning to gather herself up. 'Come and kiss me "Goodnight" children.' Lucy and Jane pecked at the crinkly white cheek, then kissed the aunts. They watched as the procession left the drawing room. Uncle Dolly tossed back his cloak revealing a red silk lining and put out an arm to escort his mother and together they took the lead, Henry bringing up the rear.

'He's allowed to stay up for dinner on a Friday night now,' Lucy explained. '*We* can read until eight o'clock, then Ivy will bring us a glass of milk and do our hair. She used to be our nursery maid and Grandma kept her on as a kindness. She's bad tempered. I don't like her.'

Jane was wondering what 'do our hair' involved.

Clothes folded away tidily, they were in capacious cotton nightdresses, then they sipped their milk and listened to Ivy's sharp comments while she brushed their hair.

'I've never seen hair so straight,' she said disapprovingly, looking at Jane in the mirrored reflection of the walnut dressing table. 'Lucky we've got some extra rags.'

Her hair was divided into strands and each wound torturously into little screws, knotted up by pieces of rag. Jane looked at herself in the mirror. She didn't care *what* she would look like as long as she could just stay.

Ivy, pixie-faced, had rough hands, winding, tying, separating the strands, more winding, tying . . . Jane closed her eyes. Lucy was chattering away but she hardly heard her. Lucky Lucy having everything done for her, everything planned for her, such a happy and uncomplicated life . . . living here with this perfect family . . . A sudden brisk tap on the head meant that Ivy had finished.

Snuggling down into the soft feather bed, Jane felt herself floating away; the lavender-smelling sheets had been warmed by a hot wrapped brick.

'I may tell you a secret tomorrow,' Lucy whispered after Ivy had lowered the gas lights and said 'goodnight'. She yawned and soon Jane heard her soft regular breathing.

'Please don't let me wake up tomorrow and find I'm "me" again,' she prayed. 'Let this go on for ever.' She tried hard to push to the back of her mind her mother's squeezing hug at the bus station and how strained her tired face had looked when she'd said, 'I've had a letter from your father – he wants you to go and live with him. But it's up to you – you're the only one who can make the decision.'

There was a faint sound, it may have been a bird in the chimney, or the bubbling of the bathroom geyser, or someone sobbing.

Chapter 4

Lucy had already gone to her Saturday dancing class at Miss Primrose's, clutching her bronze-coloured slippers, when Uncle Dolly found Jane poring over some embroidery in the drawing room.

Aunt Flora's fidgety fingers trembled as she tried to show Jane one or two stitches on a small square of creased linen. A strong scent of lavender exuded from Aunt Flora – even her breath smelt of it as she muttered, half to herself, 'no, that's not the way . . . I suppose dear Muriel hasn't the time . . . I never blamed her, you know . . . never . . .'

Jane said nothing, it was none of her business; she didn't want to be drawn into any discussion on Grace's home life. She was only thankful that Grace herself hadn't materialised. When she had awoken that morning, she had been just conscious of a feeling of relief to find that nothing had changed. She was still in the soft feather bed – everything was peaceful and calm. She struggled into petticoat, a white high-necked shirt and dark full skirt. After a breakfast of creamy porridge and a wonderful choice of bacon, scrambled eggs, sausages, kidneys, a fish and rice dish or kippers in the dining room, Lucy had taken a spoon of some nasty-looking dark brown medicine. 'Grandma says I have a weak chest,' she had explained as she and Jane went to clean their teeth in the giant wash basin in their bathroom; the bath was deep with brass taps and clawed feet.

'I've never seen a bathroom like this,' Jane had said truthfully.

'No – well, I don't suppose your father . . .' But politeness or something had made Lucy break off suddenly, embarrassed. She changed the subject. 'Look, I'll show you one of my secrets . . . It's not the main one but not even Henry knows,' and she had drawn up a delicate gold chain from round her neck. A tiny locket was attached. Jane touched the fine design engraved between minute pearls. 'It's lovely.'

Lucy had scratched the side of the locket with a finger nail and it had sprung open. 'Grandma gave it to me for my birthday with her photograph inside but I took it out and put this one in instead.' Her voice had dropped to a whisper as Jane craned forward to look. She'd seen the profile of a young, sweet-faced woman – the photograph was faded, brownish. 'Who is it?'

'My mother.' Jane could hardly hear her now. 'Aunt Flora gave it to me secretly. She was taken . . . my mother.'

'Mmm – it's nice.' Jane hadn't really known what to say. 'You mean she's . . .'

'I think she had a weak chest too. Aunt Flora said something once . . . She may have been consumptive or perhaps it was a weak heart. I don't know.'

'Why don't you ask around? Pin someone down and get a bit of info?' Jane had said vaguely, studying her own reflection in the bathroom mirror with some pleasure. Her ringlets, caught up at the back in a red bow, suited her.

'Ssh . . . Someone's coming.' Lucy had snapped the locket shut quickly. 'Don't say anything to anyone.' Her eyes had looked scared as the landing floor had creaked with footsteps.

It had only been Ivy, who had scolded them for leaving the cold water tap dripping.

Grandma had not appeared at breakfast – people had come and gone as they pleased and then the house was quiet again, everyone busy about their own affairs.

Now Uncle Dolly was shattering the quiet with his booming voice. 'Just the ticket! Just the ticket.'

Aunt Flora twitched as if she'd had an electric shock. 'Dolly, I wish you wouldn't do that – you know how my nerves . . . I've got one of my headaches coming on. I think perhaps I'd better go and take a little something . . .'

'You do that, my dear,' Uncle Dolly said in a kindly way. He went over to the potted plants and Jane saw him open up his stars and moons box while Aunt Flora wove her way through the furniture to the door, leaving a trail of her heady scent behind her.

'Now, I need an assistant for my magic show. Henry's no good these days, head in a book all the time – overworking if you ask me. What d'you think about the idea?'

'About Henry overworking? Well, I suppose if he's got exams . . .' Jane said.

'No, no,' Uncle Dolly shouted, 'what I mean is what d'you think about the idea of being my *assistant*?'

'Thanks, but I don't think I'd be any good – Mum always says I'm ham-fisted. I dropped a digi box at school,' Jane said, then bit her lip. For a moment she'd forgotten but Uncle

Dolly hadn't noticed anything. He frowned and said, 'Non-sense! You'll be perfectly splendid.'

In the green gloom of the conservatory long tendrils of ivy, twined with a vine, hung down blocking out some of the light from the glass roof. It looked mysterious, and just the place for some magic.

'Now, I'd like you to help first of all with this.' He produced from a pocket a pot of glue, which, when opened, smelt unpleasantly fishy. From another pocket he drew a small grey bag. He emptied the contents – fragments of china and glass – on to the table with a clatter. Jane looked at the chipped and broken pieces spread out like the patterns in a kaleidoscope. As if from the air Uncle Dolly now plucked an egg – he fingered it with great care and Jane could see why; at one end there was a hole – it was just a shell.

'Bantam's eggs – just the right shape. What I want you to do is stick these pieces all over the egg, as smoothly as possible and then I'll explain why.'

Gingerly Jane fingered a bit of blue and white china and started her work while Uncle Dolly busied himself arranging his props.

A brisk wind was getting up outside – it caught up beech and elm leaves, whisking them around in a whirlpool, then scattering them at random. Glancing out through the potted plants, Jane saw a boy, thin and ragged as a scarecrow, chasing them with a broom. A post boy came up the drive and stopped for a brief chat. Some of the envelopes he carried loosely in his hand were caught by a sudden gust and flew in all directions.

There was a tap-tapping across the hall floor and Grandma

appeared in the drawing room. She rapped her stick down hard on the floor. 'The post is late.'

Uncle Dolly stopped what he was doing. 'Only five minutes, mother.'

'He's just talking to the boy sweeping the leaves,' Jane chipped in. She realised with a slight shock that brown eyes are not always warm and soft. They could be hard as pebbles, like Grandma's were just then. 'Where is Flora?'

Uncle Dolly glanced briefly at Jane and said, 'She had one of her headaches and went to lie down.'

'I see.' Grandma's lips were drawn into a small tight line.

Jessie knocked at the door and brought in the post on a small silver tray, which Grandma took silently and sifted through. The minute Jessie had closed the door behind her, Grandma, while still studying the names on the envelopes, said in a low voice, 'That boy, Sam Wills. I pay him to work here, not waste time talking – he's a slacker, no good, whatever Flora may say . . . just like his father . . .'

Jane heard Uncle Dolly give an almost imperceptible sigh as Grandma left the room. 'Back to work,' he said.

'Is Sam the boy whose father stole the silver?' Jane asked, remembering what Lucy had told her.

'Ssh – we never mention such things – very uncharitable.' Uncle Dolly put a chubby finger to his lips.

Jane shrugged her shoulders. She didn't want to know any details, she was quite happy not to be involved. She finished her strange task and held up the small coated egg shell, heavy now.

'Perfectly splendid!' Uncle Dolly said and reached for a small black bag made of a satiny material. 'Now, where's my watch?' He lifted a fine silver chain, which fell in a loop on the front of his waistcoat, and out of a small pocket he drew out the same small silver ball that Jane had found in the magic box in the dumb waiter. He showed it to her, pressing the tiny switch at the top. Oh *no*, it's going to whiz me back again and I don't want to go, she thought with panic. She turned away, hearing again the tiny tinkling tune. This time Uncle Dolly was singing along to it in a soft, deep bass voice:

Backward, turn backward,
O Time, in your flight . . .
Forward, fast forward
Just for one night . . .

'Look. Have you ever seen a watch like it? Goes for seven days without winding. Finest thin silver, said to have been given to a Tsar by a member of our royal family. My father left it to me in his will. "A thing of beauty is a joy forever" – that's what he used to say. He collected beautiful things.'

Jane forced herself to turn round and look at it again.

'Seems to have stopped!' He sounded puzzled.

She closed her eyes as he attempted to wind it but the switch seemed to be stuck. I must have broken it, Jane thought guiltily.

'Drat! The spring's gone. However did that happen? I shall have to take it to Jessops this afternoon.' He snapped the watch shut. 'Never mind, we can still do our trick. You have here before you, a watch of delicate beauty. I am about to place it in this bag.' He dropped the watch into the black satin and showed Jane.

'Now, you're sure it's safely inside, aren't you?' Jane nodded her head, after checking again. He closed the bag and placed it on the table. She could see the shape of the watch quite clearly.

'Where did I put that . . .?' He burrowed under the fronds of a palm and triumphantly produced a hammer. He raised it up . . .

'And now, ladies and gentlemen, I think I shall have to dispose of my watch – it doesn't work any more. It is of no use to me now—'

Dramatically, he stopped with the hammer in mid air. 'One . . . Two . . .'

Jane could see that he intended to smash the watch into fragments. With that broken into smithereens, she would never get home again ever, even if she wanted to. Her chance would be gone. She felt terrified – the decision had come too soon and she didn't want to have to decide yet.

'Stop!' she yelled and pulled at his arm but it was too late.

'Three!' He brought his arm down smartly and she heard the horrible crash as it struck the round shape of the watch. She looked stricken but he just laughed. She couldn't explain her panic. She felt suddenly sick.

Unconcerned, Uncle Dolly waved the wand. 'Do you remember the magic words?'

Jane just shook her head, stunned.

'Dolly, jolly, zambo!'

With a deft movement, he picked up the black bag and opened it with thumbs stretched out. 'Take a look.'

Jane peered inside and there was the watch, unbroken, good as new. She took it out carefully, not able to explain to Uncle Dolly why she was so relieved.

'Not so dusty, eh?' He was pleased that she had reacted to his little trick so strongly.

'Brilliant! You should be on the—' she almost said 'telly' but changed it to 'stage'.

For a moment, it seemed as if a thundercloud had covered the sun. Jolly Uncle Dolly had become a frightening stranger. 'You're quite right of course,' he said angrily, 'I should have been . . . I wanted to be, but . . .'

But she didn't want to hear about his ambitions and how they'd been thwarted. 'Tell me how you did that trick. I saw the watch, I heard the crunch . . .'

He brightened up. 'Easy. An illusion you see, my dear – just an illusion, like so much else,' and he turned the bag upside down. From a concealed inner pocket there fell on to the table a clatter of glass, china and egg shell.

'The bantam's egg!'

'Precisely. A case of substitution – the egg for the watch, immediately after you had had a last look in the bag. The watch went round my fingers and up in to my sleeve: at the same time, the egg was deposited in the secret pocket.'

'But I didn't see any of that.'

'An illusion – things aren't always what they seem, are they? All done in the twinkling of an eye.' He demonstrated in deft slow motion how the watch could be picked up, palmed in his hand and made to disappear up the sleeve of his jacket, where it was prevented from falling out again by a piece of wadding, and brought down again at the end of the trick.

'I'm afraid I'll need another patchwork egg, if you would be so kind.' He produced one from his mouth and handed it to Jane.

Ivy, having tapped at the door, entered with a warm drink for Uncle Dolly. There was a slip of cheap pink paper folded beside it, which he picked up and read. He looked puzzled then slipped the note into his pocket.

'Thank you, Ivy.'

He sipped his drink. 'Hot milk, brandy and nutmeg – delicious beverage!' and then, as Jane returned to the glue and glass, he said, 'Excuse me, my dear, I have to slip out for a while. I hope you have a good appetite for lunch today . . . it's steak pudding.'

A baker's cart had drawn up outside – Jane could hear the baker's boy whistling a cheerful tune as he struggled with a large basket through a side gate. She finished pasting the last piece of china on the egg, placed it carefully on the table and wondered what she was meant to do next. It was the first time she'd been on her own. The room felt warm with the log fire and now the sun was streaming through the windows and the glass of the conservatory, it was almost stuffy. She decided to go out into the garden for some fresh air.

As she passed through the dark hall, the door of the morning room shut quietly; she heard the soft murmur of voices. Far away upstairs, a stair creaked. Just for a moment she felt a little tremor run through her and remembered how, whenever she shivered like that, her mother would laugh and ask, 'Someone's just walked over your grave?' Then the soothing peace and security of the house and family flooded back over her.

She was having a lovely time – I don't have to worry about a single thing, she thought. She pulled open the front door and ran down the steps into the sunlight.

It was strange to see the garden looking neat with clipped hedges and mown grass instead of the scrubby patch in front of Billa's room.

Sam was bending over a rockery, attractive with sandstone and tiny plants. He didn't look up when Jane said 'Hello' but went on collecting stray leaves. He seemed all arms and legs, his clothes were ragged and it was difficult to tell his age.

'I'll help you, if you want.' Jane started to gather up some twigs. As she crouched, he straightened up, slowly, like an old man, as if his bones were aching, and turned to stare at her. He might have been eleven or sixteen. His face, despite the nature of his job, was pale.

'Clear off, want to land me in trouble?' His voice was gruff, he looked surly. Jane remembered Grandma's words – slack, no good . . . just like his father. . . . and his dad went round nicking things. Well, she wouldn't bother to help him. 'Suit yourself,' she said.

As she backed away, her foot caught in the hem of her long skirt and she fell over one of the stones in the rockery and dislodged it, landing awkwardly on the gravel.

A pair of surprisingly strong hands yanked her to her feet. 'Now, look what you've gone an' done.'

They both looked at the stone. It was a rosy pink colour, pitted with tiny sea shells and pretty delicate white plants. Sam heaved it up ready to put it back in place, but where it had lain undisturbed, was now a seething mass of squirming grubs and worms, writhing dementedly, furious at being disturbed. 'Yuck!' Jane made a face in distaste and looked while Sam replaced the stone. Glancing at the panes of glass on the outside of the conservatory, she caught sight of her reflection, hardly recognising herself: she saw Sam, the shrubs lining the short front path and the open gate and beyond that, a figure, dressed all in black, stood there silent and watchful. She turned round quickly but it seemed to have melted away, she might almost have imagined it.

'Did you see that?' she asked Sam, although he was still trying to repair the damage to the little rock plants, patting the soil round them carefully with practised fingers.

'See what?' His voice sounded like a growl and he didn't turn round.

At that moment there was a furious tapping on one of the windows. Grandma was beckoning to her to come inside. Well, she'd be glad to. Sam was no company. 'You're a real pain – d'you know that?'

'Sticks an' stones . . .' she heard him say as she ran off.

Grandma's face was impassive and her voice level as she asked, 'What were you doing out there in the garden?'

'I was just messing about.'

'Messing about? What sort of language is that? Now understand this, my dear. While you are under my roof, I am responsible for you. I dare say Muriel may not mind you talking to riff raff but that sort of behaviour is not encouraged at The Laurels. The boy Sam comes from a very feckless family and is only here on sufferance – a kindly whim of Flora's. He lives down by the docks, a breeding ground for all manner of disease . . . typhoid, consumption . . . and I shouldn't be at all surprised if he had lice in his hair! We have to remember Lucy's delicate health.' All this warning was unnecessary, Jane thought Sam rude and horrible.

Grandma pursed her lips. 'Just look at your hair and is that soil on your dress? And we were hoping to arrange a little treat this afternoon!'

Although not altogether sure what she had done, Jane found herself feeling guilty, but only for a moment.

Grandma's lips were now strained upwards in a small tight smile. 'I suppose we can't really expect you to know any better. Perhaps we were expecting too much of you considering your background . . . Go along now and wash your hands and tidy yourself up for luncheon. Walk slowly, don't run.'

When Lucy arrived back from Miss Primrose's, the gong sounded for lunch. 'Steak pudding and treacle tart!' Uncle Dolly rubbed his hands together appreciatively.

The Vicar, the Reverend Spode, was lunching with them and said a few words of a foreign language in a deep voice before they sat down. 'He always says a Latin grace,' whispered Lucy.

Talk was of The Waifs and Strays committee and the appalling plight of the poor in Liverpool and what could be done to help.

'I hope,' Grandma said, 'we in this family do what we can to help with this truly dreadful problem. They have my heartfelt sympathy – poor things.'

'No one, could do more, dear lady,' the Reverend Spode said, washing down his biscuit and stilton cheese with a drink of port.

The girls and Henry had kept silent during the meal. Henry looked thoughtful and far away but perhaps, Jane thought, that frown and the way his mouth turned down at the corners slightly was his normal look – she didn't know him well enough to know. His expression didn't alter when Grandma said, 'We have a little treat for you this afternoon, Lucy. You and Jane can have a visit to the Palm House at Sefton Park with your Aunt Lallie. Henry, you will have to stay behind on this occasion, with your books, I'm afraid. Exams,' she explained to the Vicar, who said, 'Quite, quite.'

Lucy said, 'Thank you, Grandma.'

A strange look flickered across Aunt Lallie's face and then vanished. 'I promised Beatrice I'd go and sit with her this afternoon.'

'Your friend Beatrice seems to have too many demands on your attention, Lallie. You can quite easily see her tomorrow.'

'I'll go with the girls,' Aunt Flora said a little breathlessly.

'I thought you were having one of your headache days,' Grandma replied evenly.

'Oh, it's quite better now,' and she laughed a funny little laugh.

'You look quite flushed, dear. I think perhaps you may be getting one of your throats. An afternoon indoors will do you much more good.'

There was a short pause, broken by the Reverend Spode. 'What lucky girls – a visit to the Palm House!'

Jane thought it sounded deadly dull but kept quiet. He turned to look at her with protruding gooseberry-green eyes. 'And how is your mother, my dear?'

For the first time, Jane forgot. The question had taken her by surprise. 'She's hoping to get this new job at the King's Head in Weston. Fingers crossed and all that, that she gets it!' Then she remembered.

There was a shocked silence. Then Grandma, after clearing her throat two or three times, murmured something vaguely about 'difficult times' and 'thankful that we can help with . . .' with a meaningful look at Jane.

'You are indeed a true Christian and will reap your rewards – be in no doubt of that. And now, I'm afraid I must be going.'

'Won't you join us for a cup of China tea in the drawing

room?' said Grandma, but he shook his head, rose from the table and said another short grace.

They left the room, discussing the forthcoming concert, the current cost of replacing the church silver and Grandma's benevolence in employing the wretched Sam.

'Why did you say that about your mother? Was it true?' Lucy asked later.

'Sort of.'

'Why does everyone call her "poor Muriel"?'

'I've no idea,' Jane said honestly.

They were in Lucy's bedroom, getting ready for their outing. Jane was fumbling with tiny buttons in a pair of cream kid gloves which felt tight, like an extra skin. The clothes she'd arrived in had been folded neatly away onto the top shelf of a cupboard together with her trainers and now Lucy was sorting out pairs of buttoned boots for Jane to try on.

'Look.' But instead of boots, she reappeared from the dark inner recesses of the wardrobe clutching a biscuit tin. 'This is my other secret, in here.'

'You're secretly addicted to chocolate biscuits,' Jane guessed.

'Wrong!'

Lucy lifted off the lid very carefully. There were small holes in the top. Inside was a small white rat.

'Uncle Dolly used to use him in some of his tricks – he said I could have it as a pet but nobody must know, especially Grandma. Everyone thinks it lives in the stables and that Sam looks after it. I call him Wilfred – Wilf.' Wilf's nose was pink and twitchy, his eyes were pink too and almost luminous. Lucy stroked him gently.

'It can't be much fun for him, shut away in a biscuit tin in your wardrobe!' Jane said.

'Sshh,' Lucy put her finger to her mouth as they heard a creak on the stair. There was no further sound but her voice sank to a whisper. 'He gets a little exercise in the stable loft sometimes. I pretend I'm going to give a sugar lump to Bess, our horse, but really I play with Wilf for five minutes and get fresh hay for his bed. I daren't spend any longer or Miss Norris comes to look for me.'

Jane stroked Wilf's silken, white fur. 'What does he eat?'

'I put bits of bread or pastry into a handkerchief at meal times. No one notices, then I give them to him later.'

Those moments with her pet in the stable loft must be the only times Lucy ever has to herself. Every other minute there would be someone telling her what to do. It was all very well having things planned for you, Jane thought, but perhaps it could be like being in a biscuit tin 'prison' too. Maybe it wouldn't suit me, people watching you all the time . . . no freedom . . . no space.

Now there were more creakings – footsteps coming along the landing. Terrified, Lucy put back the lid on the biscuit tin and hurriedly pushed it back into the wardrobe.

Aunt Lallie came into the bedroom. She didn't look pleased. 'Aren't you ready yet?'

'I'm looking for my gloves,' Lucy said breathlessly and opened the top drawer of her dressing table.

Jane had managed to squeeze her feet into a pair of Lucy's boots and her toes felt bunched up. She raised her right foot and rested it on the window seat to fasten the buttons, while Lucy and Aunt Lallie rummaged through the drawer looking for gloves.

'I think it's going to rain. My wrists always ache when there's rain about and they're aching now.' Aunt Lallie was grumbling more to herself than anyone else.

There was a good view from this window high up in the house. Looking out to see if the rain had already started, Jane pressed her nose to the glass. No sign of Sam now in the front garden but smoke drifting from a bonfire partly obscured the figure of a woman dressed in black standing by the front gate, a heavy veil covering her face. She was looking up at the window and, seeing Jane, raised an arm slightly, as if in recognition. Then a large puff of smoke billowed round, concealing her, and when it cleared, she had gone.

Chapter 5

Jane drew back quickly. Did the woman think she was Grace?

'Come along!' Aunt Lallie shouted irritably.

Downstairs, they opened the front door. Puffs of smoke made Lucy cough and they hurried along to avoid it. There was no sign of any figure in black but a man, with a monkey wearing a red waistcoat, on his shoulders, was turning the handle of a barrel organ, which produced tinkling, jerky music.

'That's the "Moon and Stars" waltz from the "Desert Rose" . . . The one Ivy's always humming. She goes to the Music Hall,' Lucy said as she and Jane stopped to look at the monkey. The monkey stared back and put out a skinny paw. Jane went to stroke him but was pulled away.

'Fleas,' hissed Aunt Lallie but she popped a coin into a cap lying on the ground. The church clock struck three.

'Three o'clock already!' Aunt Lallie seemed agitated. 'And there's so much . . .' But she didn't go on.

The road led on to a wide tree-lined avenue, with similar huge houses standing proudly behind clipped hedges. Trams rattled along, drawn by horses: a few smart carriages pulled by horses passed by and a boy with a large brush was busy, dodging the traffic, sweeping away leaves and horse manure.

Lucy and Jane were bustled through the large iron gates of the park.

'I'll take you to the Palm House and you'll have to amuse yourselves there for a while. You'll be perfectly all right . . . and no need to mention this to anyone.' As they hurried along, Aunt Lallie checked through some papers she'd brought in her bag.

'Here we are.' She hurried them into the large, hot and humid greenhouse, riffling through her papers again, not noticing that two escaped, drifting gently on to a large bamboo before fluttering down on to the damp tiles. Giving a vague wave, she hurried away.

Jane looked round. A couple of gardeners were busy opening vents and watering the plants, some exotic and colourful but mostly green.

'Boring,' Jane pronounced as they walked round avoiding puddles, 'really boring.'

They sat on a bench, near where they had been abandoned and, for something to do, Jane reached down and retrieved the two pieces of paper Aunt Lallie had dropped. They were damp.

Smoothing one out, Jane read out loud: '"We are hoping to have the honour of welcoming Mrs Pankhurst at our next meeting to be held at the home of our secretary, Miss Beatrice Allenby, The Grove, Upper Park Crescent on the 27th of this month. Your presence is requested. Your attendance will be vitally important to our cause . . . Women Unite!" Just a stupid old leaflet and the other one is exactly the same. Some needlework group or a tea party.'

'It must be important to her, though,' Lucy said. 'I wonder if Grandma knows about it.'

'I shouldn't think so somehow.' Jane crumpled the leaflets up and stuffed them into a pocket. 'Why should we be stuck in here? I'm suffocating. Let's go and explore the park. Is that a lake over there?'

Lucy bunched up her skirt and ran with surprising speed, flying along like a bird released from its cage. Jane chased her and they had a game of tick across the grass until, laughing and exhausted, they stopped by the water. Ducks came waddling up to meet them.

'They're always hungry. I've got some crumbs from lunch I saved for Wilf.' Lucy felt in one of her pockets and scattered some around. Two swans glided by. 'They want some too.' She stood on a steep, raised bank and vigorously hurled some bits into the lake but lost her balance on the wet grass. Before she could save herself, she ended up in the water, gasping and choking as she came up for air.

'Lucy!' Jane screamed and splashed after her.

Although the water wasn't too deep, it was icy and smelly. Lucy was panicking – her arms flailed wildly as Jane tried to grab her. She seemed to be sinking in the mud, fighting and spluttering.

'Keep still, can't you?' Jane shouted and made a desperate effort to cling on to her, heaving and pulling with all her strength until she managed to drag Lucy out, shocked, soaked and covered with slimy green weeds.

As Jane took off her coat to wrap round the shivering Lucy, she knew there was going to be big trouble, a hundred times more trouble than if it had happened out with Mum or Billa, who might have just laughed and told her not to be so silly before bundling her home.

They started back towards the Palm House and in the distance saw Aunt Lallie coming across the park, doing her best to run in her heavy clothes.

She reached them, out of breath, and took in the situation quickly. 'Great heavens! You wretched children,' she gasped. 'I only turned my back for two minutes and this happens.'

She'd been gone ages, Jane thought and she looked ugly with fright and anger, her brows drawn together. She took off her pleated cape with its fur trimmings and muffled Lucy up in it. 'Come on, come on, hurry up!' They ran awkwardly, stumbling in clinging, damp, unwieldy skirts back to The Laurels and through the back door, all of them shivering, the girls still dripping.

'Sshh!' Aunt Lallie put a warning finger up to her lips.

In the kitchen, Mrs Murphy was dozing in front of the range and was snoring softly but just as they reached the top of the stairs, which led to the hall, Ivy came through, balancing a tray on her hip. She gave them all a sharp surprised look.

'Well, I never! Miss Lucy you look frozen to death. You're wet too! Whatever will your grandmother say?' She tried to sound concerned but looked pleased.

'That's enough, Ivy. We just got caught in a sudden squall. Bring us some heated bricks for the girls' beds and hot soup – quickly please.' Ivy pushed past and the others crept through the hall and up the main staircase.

'Into bed. I'll dry your clothes in front of my bedroom fire. Have a rest before your tea. No one must know.' Aunt Lallie left their room.

'She seems seriously worried,' Jane said.

'She left us alone,' Lucy said simply.

'She left us alone and then went off somewhere by herself – mmmm, I wonder where.'

'Something to do with that leaflet we found?'

'Perhaps she was delivering—' but Jane broke off as Ivy pushed open the door and put the wrapped bricks in their beds.

'You can have some soup with your supper. I'm not coming up again for you two madams – and what mischief have you been getting into, I'd like to know, dripping all over the kitchen stairs?' But there was no reply and she went out banging the door behind her.

'I don't like Ivy,' Lucy said.

'I shouldn't think anyone does.'

'Yes, they do. She has a gentleman friend called Arthur. He takes her to the Music Hall on her night off. That's what Jessie told me. We sometimes talk together when Jessie's dusting if no one's listening. She's nice.'

'Well, perhaps Ivy's had a bust up with Arthur. That's why she's such a pain. I think I heard her crying last night. Her room's overhead, isn't it?'

'No, the Tower Room is overhead, I told you. No one goes in there – it's kept locked and, anyway, Ivy's always like that. You must have imagined someone crying.'

Lucy fell asleep but Jane didn't feel like resting. I'll just creep quietly out of the bedroom and go and have a little look round on my own, she decided.

It was dark on the landing even in the daytime – no gas lights until the evening. There was no sound from Henry's room – probably has his head in a book, poor thing, she thought.

The small staircase she'd noticed before seemed to pull her like a magnet. The stairs were quite steep but there was an elegant curved banister and rail to hold on to. The staircase curved round as it went up into the dark. As she crept up the stairs her eyes became accustomed to the gloom, and she could just see a solid door in front of her. The room behind it must be over their bedroom.

One of the floorboards creaked under her feet and at the same time Jane heard a faint echoing creak, which might have come from the other side of the door. Feeling carefully with her fingers, she found a brass knob. Very softly, she turned it and pushed but, as Lucy had said, it was locked. Below the handle she felt a keyhole and, bending down, she peered through. There was something blocking her view. Frustrated, she poked at it with her finger and looked again and realised what it was. A key. The door must be locked from the inside. That's really strange.

Suddenly there were brisk footsteps which could be heard coming up the lower stairs and along the corridor to the bedroom she and Lucy shared.

'Lucy! Jane!' It was Aunt Lallie.

Jane froze back against the wall. She had the feeling, without quite knowing why, that she shouldn't be up there, fiddling with the key of the locked room. She heard Lucy say, 'she's probably gone to the bathroom'.

'Are you sure you're feeling warm and rested now?' Aunt Lallie's voice sounded worried, 'and as I said before, no need to mention your little . . . adventure. We wouldn't want to upset Grandma, would we? Put on your tartan dress when you get up. We have visitors coming this evening for some music and you and Jane can stay up a little later than usual and join us – that will be nice, won't it?' And she left the room and went to speak to Henry.

Quickly, stealthily, Jane picked her way down the stairs, went into the bathroom and came out again closing the door noisily.

'Oh, there you are,' Lucy said as Jane came back into the bedroom. 'I asked Aunt Lallie's permission this morning to take you to the stable to see Bess. But really we can take Wilf for some exercise in the loft. Sam's made a little run for him out of chicken wire.'

Sam? thought Jane. So he can't be all bad.

She chose a blue velvet dress of Lucy's which was too tight for her so she left the back buttons undone and slipped on a silk jacket. She helped Lucy into her tartan dress and asked, 'Don't you have any casuals? Tops, trousers, to muck around in? No, you don't have a clue of what I'm talking about, do you? You never muck around.'

'I don't think I want to – it doesn't sound very nice. Anyway, don't you have any dresses for formal occasions? You didn't bring any clothes with you except that awful tatty fur . . . thing.'

Jane thought for a minute. She seemed to remember that in the very distant past, she had once owned a pretty pink dress, handed on to her from a friend of her mother's, whose daughter had outgrown it. Jane had only worn it once, for someone's party.

She laughed when she saw Lucy looking bewildered. 'Come on, fetch Wilf and we'll give him some freedom.'

With a jacket covering the large tin, they went downstairs, through the hall and down the back stairs to the door which led to the cobbled yard at the rear of the house.

'Nice smell,' Jane said as they entered the stable.

'Hay.'

Bess, the chestnut horse, was enjoying her meal of oats from a nosebag. She took no notice of the girls as they climbed steps up to the loft.

'You are lucky, having a horse. When do you ride her?' Jane asked.

'I don't ride her, silly. Bess is our carriage horse. I go for riding lessons in the park sometimes. Be careful, Jane, you nearly dropped Wilf then.'

It wasn't easy clutching Wilf's tin and trying not to trip over the full skirts.

'We should have brought a candle but Ivy would have wanted to know why we needed one.' Lucy said, as Wilf's tin with the lid open was put into the middle of the square of chicken wire and placed on its side. The rat was out in a trice, exploring his new larger prison.

Toys had been improvised for him in the shape of a newspaper ball, a cardboard base with a hole and an old cocoa tin, which Wilf was now rolling around. The girls sat down on a pile of old horse blankets.

'Look at that – isn't he clever?' but Jane was not watching Wilf's antics. By the poor light from a skylight in the roof she could see that this was no ordinary stable loft. Her eyes became used to the gloom.

'This is fantastic . . . amazing!' They were surrounded by pieces of intricately carved furniture, oriental curios, brass musical instruments, painted masks and much more.

'What a great place for a party!' Jane said.

'What do you mean, "place for a party"? These are all grandfather's treasures. He was in shipping – the Patterson

Line and did a lot of travelling. Everything is catalogued. Grandfather Patterson was a very great man.' Lucy said all this as if it was something she had been taught, like a recitation. Family pride, I suppose, thought Jane. Well, a good thing to have.

'All this should be in a museum – you could charge people to come and have a look.'

'Grandmother would never allow anyone to touch these things. They're very precious.' She ran her fingers over a brass gong, which was placed in the lap of a golden Buddha, who had half-closed eyes and an unpleasant smile on his face. 'This was given to grandfather by the King of Siam,' Lucy said proudly.

Glad to get rid of it, I expect, Jane thought to herself, banging the gong with her fist. It made a surprisingly loud boom which echoed round the loft. 'Sshh,' Lucy put a finger to her lips.

The painted masks and carved heads appeared to be leering down at the two girls. Strange shadows were cast by the antique curios.

Something brushed against Jane's face with a light silken caress. Hanging from a beam by a thread, a large cobweb was swaying slightly and was now sticking to her skin as she tried to pull it away. 'Ugghh!'

'We must go – quickly.' Lucy picked up Wilf and popped him into his tin, closing the lid.

Jane picked up the urgency in Lucy's voice and the two of them, Jane clutching the tin, hurried as fast as they could down the steps, past Bess, who was kicking her hooves at the side of her stall.

Once back in the hall, silent apart from the ticking of the

grandfather clock, they caught their breath and dusted themselves down and were about to climb the main stairs when a door opened softly.

'Where are you two going?' Grandmother came out of the drawing room and confronted them with a sharp, suspicious look.

Jane hurriedly concealed the tin with the jacket. 'Lucy has just been showing me your horse – Aunt Lallie said she could.' Well, it wasn't a complete lie and why would she need to lie anyway? Why had she felt guilty for a moment? Why couldn't she have said, 'We've just been giving Wilf some exercise and, by the way, I think those bits and pieces in the loft are amazing.' But somehow she knew she couldn't. She could sense Lucy, tense behind her, as Grandmother's eyes alighted on the jacket but at that moment there was a diversion. Aunt Flora, appearing at the top of the stairs, seemed to lose her footing and with a cry, collapsed in a miserable heap a little lower down, with her head against the banister.

Jane pushed the tin into Lucy's arms and ran up the stairs two at a time, hearing a tearing sound coming from her petticoat as her shoe caught in a frill. She put an arm round Aunt Flora. 'Are you OK? Have you broken anything?'

Aunt Flora raised a flushed face. 'Perfectly all right dear, thank you . . . I just . . . it was just . . . so silly of me. Please don't make a fuss.' Her eyes looked pleading. Trembling and wobbling, she managed to stand up. 'See, I'm quite all right.' She was speaking to Grandmother, who stood still as a marble statue then spoke in a cold, disapproving voice. 'You must be more . . . careful.'

'I know, I'm sorry, mother. I can't—'

'Never mind that. The Calverts and Braithwaites will be arriving at half past eight for our soirée – perhaps you'd better go and practise your Chopin. And you two,' she looked at the girls, 'will be joining us this evening, so best behaviour, please – and Lucy, you may give us a recitation.' This was said as if bestowing a privilege. Then she withdrew back into the drawing room. Treading gingerly, Flora passed Jane and Lucy and followed her mother.

Back in their bedroom, Lucy deposited Wilf in the back of the wardrobe and Jane tore off the piece of torn frill.

'What's a swarray?' she asked.

'Don't you have them at your home? They're like little concerts but in your own house. Everyone does a turn – a song, piece of poetry or plays a musical instrument. I think it's boring but the others seem to enjoy it. We'll be expected to hand round sugar biscuits and almond cakes beforehand and everyone talks and talks . . .'

'What are you going to do?'

'A piece I've been learning with Miss Norris called *The Lady of Shallott*. Henry usually recites something like *The Charge of the Light Brigade*. She looked at Jane. 'What can you do?'

'Nothing, but I probably won't be asked.'

'No, you probably won't, being poor Muriel's daughter—' She stopped. 'I'm very sorry, I shouldn't have said that – it sounded rude. I mean – she's your mother.'

'Don't you know why she is known as "poor" Muriel?'

'No, I don't, but she always is . . . Something sad or dreadful, a long time ago but Grandmother is so good – everyone says so, and she wouldn't want you to suffer for your mother's sin – that's why she said you could come and stay.'

Big deal, thought Jane – but perhaps it was a great improvement on Grace's home life. Maybe she lived in a squalid, sordid den of thieves and it was luxuriously comfortable here. She was enjoying it herself, wasn't she? Wasn't she?

After supper, they could hear people arriving. The wind had got up and they could hear great gusts whenever the front door opened. Sash windows rattled and at half past eight, as they went down to join the others in the drawing room with Aunt Lallie, rain was lashing the stained-glass window on the landing.

All was cosy and snug in the drawing room. The plush curtains were drawn against the storm outside, the gas lights and blazing fire gave light and warmth and some friendly flickering shadows danced beyond the circle of friends.

'Ah – there you are, Lallie.' Grandmother's voice rose above the gentle murmur of voices, ushering them forward.

'You know my granddaughter, Lucy, and this—' she waved a hand in Jane's direction, 'is the daughter of a cousin of ours, staying for a few days – company for Lucy while Henry is studying hard for the entrance examination for his public school.'

While Jessie handed round small glasses of ginger wine from a tray, the two girls offered plates of biscuits and tiny cakes to the visitors, sitting or standing in little groups around the room. The women sat very upright. 'They must take ages fixing their hair,' thought Jane . . . and those lovely elaborate dresses! She was so busy just looking that she nearly emptied the plate of almond shortbread on to someone's lap.

Trying to right the plate she tipped a couple of biscuits on the carpet. 'Whoops! Oh now look what I've done!'

A pleasant young man with a large moustache took the plate from her. 'Let me assist you.'

Jane picked up the biscuits and wiped them on her dress and was suddenly aware of Grandmother frowning at her from across the room.

'Do you live hereabouts?' the young man asked.

'Oh, here, there and everywhere really,' she replied truthfully.

He looked rather taken aback. He took a biscuit, handed the plate back to Jane, then went over to talk to Grandmother.

They're talking about me, I'm sure, Jane thought, edging over to be a little nearer to where Grandma sat enthroned on her high-backed chair by the fire. Absentmindedly helping herself to the biscuits she tried to eavesdrop but the voices were low and people nearby were laughing in an animated conversation.

'Poor Muriel,' (there it was again) '. . . penniless artist . . . What can you expect . . . I do what I can . . .'

A woman, sitting on Grandma's right and listening in, said fervently, 'You're a saint, Mrs Patterson.' Grandma sighed and sipped her ginger wine.

Uncle Dolly suddenly clinked his glass with a teaspoon and the chattering stopped.

'Welcome to you all on this wild evening.' A gust of wind howled down the chimney making everyone feel snug and glad to be safely indoors.

'I'm sure we will have a very enjoyable, diverse and entertaining programme with all the fantastic talent assembled here tonight.' There was applause and laughter at this.

'I believe Miss Gwendolyne Braithwaite has volunteered to be first and foremost with a fine frolicsome piece on the piano forte entitled "Gallop".' With a rustle of purple taffeta, Miss Gwendolyne Braithwaite walked over to the piano.

'Dolly sounds quite like one of those Masters of Ceremonies they have at the Music Halls,' the woman sitting on Grandma's right said to her, 'not that I have ever been in one of those places, of course,' she added quickly.

'I should think not indeed! Disgraceful low dens of vice by all accounts. They should be closed – every one of them.' Grandma shuddered as if the very thought of them polluted her mind.

Jane, snuggling back in a velvet, button-back chair nearby, let her imagination play around the thought of these low-life Music Halls – could they really be so wicked? Then Miss Braithwaite struck up with some spirited arpeggios and she nestled into the plushy warm fabric and felt contented.

Major George Calvert, moustachioed and upright, was next with a stirring recitation called *The Death of Nelson*, which had one or two of the ladies dabbing at their eyes, and the men looking serious and proud, with patriotic fervour.

'Too long,' thought Jane.

'Miss Sybil Braithwaite will now sing in sweetest soprano a select song of sincere sentiments.'

'The rose which I give you' was sung in a weak quavering voice and Sybil Braithwaite was obviously relieved to finish it, smiling uncertainly at the polite applause.

'Come along, Lucy.' Uncle Dolly took her by the hand and she got up reluctantly from the small foot stool on which she'd been sitting hoping not to be noticed.

'I'm afraid I don't know it all – I've just learnt three verses of *The Lady of Shallot* by Alfred Lord Tennyson.' Major Calvert clapped encouragingly.

'On either side the river lie
Long fields of barley and of rye
That clothe the wold and meet the sky
And through the fields . . . and through the fields
The road runs by to many towered Camelot . . .'

She only forgot her lines once. When she got to the end, Jane gave her a 'thumbs up' sign.

While poor Aunt Flora was stumbling through Chopin's Minute waltz (it was going to take at least four and a half minutes the way it was going, Jane reckoned), Uncle Dolly came over to her and whispered, 'I've left my sheet music in the morning room – be a good girl and go and fetch it for me, would you? It's from *The Mikado* by Gilbert and Sullivan, "A Wandering Minstrel" – pictures of Japanese people on the front – you can't miss it.'

Jane picked her way quietly round the audience and went into the morning room, where she saw the music lying on a table. Picking it up, the small piece of pink paper she had seen Ivy pass to Uncle Dolly on a tray with his drink earlier, fluttered down on to the carpet. It was unfolded now and Jane saw there was something scrawled there – but didn't have time to think anything of it. She put it between the sheets of music and returned to the drawing room, where Aunt Flora's fumbling fingers were still trying to cope with the last notes of the waltz.

'Here you are.' Jane handed the music to Uncle Dolly, who spotted the pink paper protruding from a corner. He swore softly, crumpled it up and threw it towards the fire but it landed on the hearth, near where Jane had her chair.

'Thank you, thank you,' Aunt Flora's voice was querulous as she rose from the piano stool. She looked uncertain as to where to go next and sat down again on the stool as Colonel Braithwaite cleared his throat.

'I have been asked by the Reverend Spode to say a few words at this stage in our delightful evening, so kindly hosted by the Patterson family. It concerns the splendid concert that is being arranged – to be held in the church hall in six weeks' time. I am sure you will give this your fullest support and purchase tickets. You must all be aware of the excellent cause for this fund raising. We are hoping to raise money so that we can eventually replace our magnificent church silver collection which vanished some years ago. It was a sad time in the history of our parish and it may take a long time before we are in a position to make up the loss. Of course, any donations will be gratefully received. It is a cause very dear to the heart of our hostess,' here, Colonel Braithwaite made a little bow to Grandma, who acknowledged it with a tight smile. 'The loss was felt most keenly by her late husband – everyone will remember his love of all things beautiful.' A murmur went round the room as people recollected Alfred Patterson.

'Adolphus has promised to give a demonstration of his magical powers at the concert, haven't you, Dolly? And I may say, one way or another, the concert should provide a great deal of pleasure for everyone. Thank you.'

After Uncle Dolly's song there was loud applause. He was announcing a recitation which Aunt Lallie was going to perform when another gust of wind sent sparks from the fire, spitting out orange and bright yellow darts. One or two came very near to the pink, crumpled paper. Not wishing to rattle the fire guard and throw it into the fire, making a noise during the announcement, Jane picked it up and put it in one of her pockets.

'I believe the poem is called *Rise of the Felines*. But I don't know who wrote it . . . perhaps the author, or authoress, wished to remain anonymous.' Aunt Lallie began.

'*Rise of the Felines*
The time is come, beware of us,
There's thunder in the air.
Your future's in the care of "us".
Beware of "us" – beware
* * *
We'll cease to coax and cozen you
By fascinating smiles
And gaily now impose on you
By dynamitic wiles.'

There was a stunned silence after this. The wind moaned in the chimney and Lallie, with a proud and now triumphant smile, went to sit down.

'What was all that about, eh? Felines, cats . . .' Colonel Braithwaite asked in his loud voice.

'Plague of tigers?' someone volunteered.

'Or something altogether more sinister,' Jane heard someone else mutter quietly. There were whispers . . . 'This emancipation nonsense', 'Double meaning for "felines" and "feminists" ', 'No surely not!'

Grandma sat rigid, two bright angry spots of colour in her cheeks the only sign of agitation. Uncle Dolly broke the tension. 'How about a song from our young guest here?' There seemed to be a general sigh of relief and Jane suddenly found herself the centre of attention. She squeezed back into her chair. 'Oh no, I don't know anything.'

But Uncle Dolly came over, took her by the hand and was leading her to the piano. Gwendolyne Braithwaite said encouragingly, 'Everyone knows *Say a little prayer for Fido.*'

'Sorry.' She glanced round the room. Grandma looked as if her mind was on something else altogether. Lucy smiled at Jane and nodded.

'Well, I've done some Karaoke at friends' discos – but I had all the words written out for me.' Uncle Dolly looked bewildered. 'Karry what?'

Then she remembered how they'd sung Beatles numbers at home a long time ago. Dad's Beatles Collection . . . Dad. No – I mustn't think of him at the moment. Well, she was in Liverpool, what better than something local?

'Penny Lane.'

A buzz of interest followed this. There could be no piano accompaniment and the rhythm would be strange to them. She was on her own.

Tapping her right foot and clapping her hands to set the pace, she gave it her best shot with her loud, clear voice:

'Penny Lane is in my ears
And in my eyes.
There beneath the blue suburban skies . . .'

Halfway through she shouted, 'Come along, everybody – clap along with me!' A young man, smart in waistcoat, watch chain and blue bow tie, tried unsuccessfully to snap his fingers in time to the rhythm but everyone else looked nervous.

'I say . . . that was a bit . . . different.' Uncle Dolly seemed almost lost for words as Jane's voice died softly away at the end. 'Penny La-a-ane.'

There was a good round of applause and some critical comments. 'Don't know what things are coming . . .'

'Never heard anything like it!'

'Remarkable.'

'It couldn't have been about that dreadful street, the wrong side of the park?'

'A Music Hall ditty?' There was a general shudder and Jane heard again the fateful words 'poor Muriel'.

'Well done, young lady. Your song was avant garde but spirited. You have a good delivery. And now . . .' Uncle Dolly raised his voice and reached for his glass of wine. 'Before carriages arrive, we must drink a toast to our Prime Minister – to Mr Gladstone!'

'Mr Gladstone,' everyone responded and drained their glasses.

'That was a strange song you sang,' Lucy said to Jane, who had come to join her on the tapestry foot stool.

'Did you like it? It sounds better with guitars and drums. I'll teach it to you, if you like.'

Lucy looked vague. 'Perhaps.'

Goodbyes were being said now. The drawing room door opened and sounds of carriage wheels and the clip clop of horses' hooves could be heard as Jessie entered with an envelope. She went straight over to Grandma. 'This arrived – special delivery, madam, about an hour ago but I didn't want to disturb you.'

Grandma's white claw-like hand shot out. Opening the envelope and adjusting her pince-nez she read the message. Jane heard her sharp intake of breath and the soft, furious yet fearful, 'they can't do this!' But no one took much notice in the polite scramble to retrieve cloaks, mufflers, hats and say, 'thank you'.

Later, while getting undressed, Jane felt the scrunch in her pocket. She took out the pink crumpled paper and straightened it out.

'I NO SUMTHIN ABOWT YOU' was written boldly but in an illiterate hand.

Lucy was asleep. The noise of the rattling sash windows drowned any sounds that might have been coming from the Tower Room that night. Snuggling down in bed, Jane thought about her day. Was she imagining Grandma's silent fury at Aunt Lallie's little poem or her tone when she'd opened the letter that had arrived? Aunt Flora seemed on edge and Uncle Dolly had lost his usual beaming smile when he'd seen the note in the pages of his music – looking cold and angry?

Was Lucy happy?

I'm probably just imagining things, she thought. I like it here. I really do . . .

Don't I?

Chapter 6

Jane awoke to the sound of church bells.

'Early service.' Lucy's voice was sleepy. 'We go to the eleven o'clock one. St Enoch's is only in Sefton Crescent but Grandma likes to take the carriage. We'll walk.'

From a distance they heard a faint sound of raised voices and a door slammed, then Ivy came in with a jug of hot water and poured it into the blue and white bowls. She looked sulky as she squeezed and buttoned the girls into Sunday best dresses and delicate leather boots.

'It's all too tight – I feel as if I can hardly breathe,' Jane complained, but Ivy was unsympathetic and brushed their hair roughly. Had Ivy herself written that note that she'd found last night? She knew what had been written but what had it meant?

At breakfast, everything seemed peaceful and normal. The well-ordered routine soothed Jane all over again.

'Henry, you're very quiet, aren't you going to favour us with a little conversation this morning?' asked Grandma.

'Perhaps he has his mind on something else, eh?' said Uncle Dolly, helping himself to a plateful of porridge from a steaming bowl on the sideboard.

'Latin and Greek?' Aunt Flora asked in a playful way but Henry didn't answer. He was a shadowy figure, Jane thought. Lucy said he used to be fun but he certainly didn't seem like that now, with his dark brows drawn together and a perpetual brooding look.

'Have you seen the newspapers this morning, Mother?' asked Uncle Dolly to change the subject.

'No and I have no desire to – they're always full of the same things – Home Rule for Ireland, the East African situation, Lord Tennyson's death . . .'

'No, there's something a little different today. Enfranchisement of women imminent in New Zealand – there! What d'you think about that!'

Jane felt as if an electric current had shot through the room, an atmosphere of shock seemed to turn everyone to stone for a moment. Enfranchisement – what does it mean? – obviously something dreadful – something unmentionable going on in New Zealand, she thought.

Grandma broke the silence. 'You surely know my views on *that*, Dolly. Your father would turn in his grave at the very thought!' Flora dropped a spoon on the floor; Lallie looked down at her plate.

'Don't you have any sympathy for the cause, Mother? I should have thought . . . it will surely arrive here one of these days . . .'

'Not another word.'

Jane and Lucy looked at each other in horror. It was going to arrive here one of these days, Uncle Dolly had said. Scary.

The wind had mostly blown itself out but it was raining and looked as if it would never stop, the sky was so leaden. Lucy sneezed.

'You'd better come in the carriage with me and your aunts this morning. Dolly, you'll walk with Henry and Jane,' Grandma said.

'Where are we going?' Jane whispered to Lucy.

'Church of course. I told you.'

There were no questions about who wanted to go – it was the family's routine: if it was Sunday morning, it was church, if it was one o'clock, it was Sunday dinner and probably a roast, Jane thought. Life at home was so haphazard, she'd never been to a church service – her mother spent Sundays catching up on all the things she hadn't done during the week. She had been on one or two school visits to ancient churches and a cathedral and had liked the quiet atmosphere and the old solid stone buildings with their feeling of permanence, like this house.

'I'll see you in church,' Lucy waved a gloved hand and went out of the front door, sheltered from the rain by a large black umbrella held by Goff. She stepped up into the carriage followed by Grandma and her two daughters and Jane, swathed in a large waterproof cape, watched them go with Bess harnessed up trotting down the road.

'They'll get there before us – why are they going so early?' she asked Uncle Dolly.

'To put fresh flowers on my father's grave.'

They walked silently through the rain along shiny pavements, sheltered under black umbrellas. On the way, people emerged from other large houses following the mournful sound of the church bell, now getting louder – just one bell being rung now.

Other carriages stopped by St Enoch's – a tall, imposing, dark stone church with a spire reaching high up to the sky surrounded by the graveyard. Up the path a crowd of people walked respectfully, then went in through a massive oak door . . . too wet to linger and talk.

Looking like a cluster of ravens, Jane spied the sombre figures of Grandma, the aunts and Lucy huddled round a large stone cross, their black umbrellas flapping slightly like wings. There were many other memorial stones, urns, broken columns, carved angels and plain slabs with engraved names but Grandfather's cross appeared to be the most impressive.

'Come along, we'll wait in the porch.' They left their umbrellas and soon Grandma came and led the small family procession down the aisle, nodding stiffly to a favoured few acquaintances.

Loud music from the organ soared up to the roof. It might have been very cold and gloomy in the huge space but it wasn't. Jane noticed some iron radiators and chrysanthemums – orange and yellow – bright stained-glass windows and the glow of gas lights, gave it a colourful glow.

'You can share my prayer book,' Lucy said in a low voice as they settled into an oak-panelled family pew near the front, 'and here's your collection,' and she pressed a silver coin into Jane's gloved hand.

The morning service wasn't familiar to her but Jane rather like the old-fashioned words, the 'Thy's and 'Thou's, and followed it in Lucy's book along with the Psalms and stirring hymns, which she mostly just mouthed. She wouldn't have been able to have made herself heard anyway as Uncle Dolly stood next to her. 'Fight the Good Fight,' he bellowed.

She knelt when Lucy knelt – on beautiful tapestry kneelers, two of which in their pew had been embroidered by Aunt Flora. 'Pictures of the old church silver, which was stolen,'

Lucy whispered. 'They—' but Grandma turned and silenced her with a warning look. Jane studied the kneelers' designs, picked out in silver thread. There was a pair of candlesticks, a crucifix, goblets and vase.

They were all seated now. From the pulpit, the Reverend Spode addressed his hushed congregation. 'For my text today, I am going to take "The sins of the fathers shall be visited yea unto the next generation. Be sure your sin will find you out." '

There was a slight disturbance further along the pew. It was the clatter of coins on the floor. It looked as if Aunt Flora had dropped her collection. With a little nervous cough and mutters of, 'I'm, sorry, I'm sorry,' she attempted to pick it all up again, even the ones which had rolled away. Her fingers faltered.

'I'll help you.' Jane got down on her hands and knees but a furious 'Leave it!' from Grandma and a disapproving 'Shhh' from the pew behind stopped them. Jane sat back and tried to concentrate on the sermon but found her mind wandering. The colours of the stained-glass windows reflected on to the white hair of an elderly man sitting in front and turned it purple. Like Billa's looked when she tried to dye it that time. She smiled at the thought. What was Billa doing? Was she missing her? She felt a pang of something – was she homesick? She couldn't be, she'd had so many homes, so many moves . . . all the same. Her gaze wandered to the windows. The one on the left looked as if it was dedicated to Grandfather Patterson: 'Sacred to the Memory.' Dates and pictures of steamships.

Someone further back gave a little snore and she turned round. Colonel Braithwaite had his eyes closed and gave another snore, then jerked to attention as his daughter nudged him.

Further back still, beyond the packed rows, Jane could see a figure standing alone by one of the columns. It was a woman dressed all in black with a veil over her face.

'Glory be to God the Father, God the Son and God the Holy Ghost.' The sermon had drawn to a close. 'Before our service ends,' the Reverend Spode said, standing before the altar, 'I have just one announcement to make. As most of you probably know, we are holding a concert in the church hall in six weeks' time to raise further money for the restoration of our church silver collection which sadly vanished from our midst some time ago. Of course, our original chalice, candlesticks and other treasures were older than our present church but we hope to be able to purchase others which will be distinguished, if not antique.

'The concert will take the form of an arena for local talent of which I am sure we have an abundance in this parish.' He paused for discreet laughter. 'So if you can sing, recite, play a musical instrument, please give your name to Miss Isobel Rathbone, who is kindly organising the programme.' There was a slight murmuring and then silence.

A hymn, during which the collection was taken, prayers for absent friends and those in need (Jane stole a look at Grandma and wondered if she was praying for 'poor Muriel'), another hymn and then Reverend Spode gave the final blessing.

Grandma and her family processed down the aisle and were first into the porch to say 'Good morning' to the Vicar.

'Such a splendid sermon, so stimulating.' Her pale lips

were stretched in her tight smile. Others pressed forward and Uncle Dolly escorted his mother, sisters and niece to their carriage.

Jane hadn't seen the veiled figure as she came out of the church but as she started to walk down the path, she struggled to put up her umbrella and out of the corner of her eye saw the woman sliding round the side of some of the older ivy-covered tombstones as if she were hiding. It was a dismal, melancholy place to be.

The rain was getting heavier, Henry had gone on ahead but turned to wait for her and the two of them caught up with Uncle Dolly and they started to walk home.

'Come on slow coaches!'

'Look, I'm sorry, Uncle Dolly. I seem to have left my prayer book behind in the church. I'll have to go back,' Henry said. 'I'll catch you up,' and he vanished round a corner before his uncle had time to reply.

The huge mansions in the crescent looked like crouching giants, Jane thought, about to gather round and form a gigantic circle for a crazy game of Ring a Roses.

The laurel bushes, which gave the house its name, were dripping. The gaunt exterior of the house looked cheerless but inside, all was warmth. Uncle Dolly vanished, Lucy was nowhere to be seen and Henry hadn't managed to catch up with them. Despite the umbrella, Jane felt soaked. She shook herself like a wet dog, fluffed out her hair and looked for somewhere to hang up the wet cape. Ivy would know where to put it and the sodden boots, which she'd taken off. She walked noiselessly across the hall.

Voices were coming from the morning room. 'Don't let me hear another word about it.' It was Uncle Dolly but he sounded somehow different, quiet, menacing and not at all jolly any more.

Then a cheeky, high-pitched voice, 'We'll see about that. We'll want a good sum for keeping our mouths shut. A hundred pounds at least!'

'Get out, get out!'

Something else, which Jane couldn't hear, was said in a low tone. She hid quickly behind the side of the grandfather clock as someone came out from the morning room, opened the door that led down to the kitchen, and slammed it behind them.

Sunday dinner, served by Jessie at one o'clock precisely, was a magnificent feast but no one seemed hungry.

'Oyster soup, your favourite, Dolly. What's the matter, are you sickening for something?' Grandma asked.

'Not at all, not at all.' He tried a little joke but Jane thought his jollity was forced.

The two aunts were subdued. Henry had nearly been late for the meal and picked at his plate of roast grouse, he hardly spoke and seemed miles away.

'Did you notice how Mrs Povey-Reeves pushed herself forward to speak to the Vicar after the service? So ill bred. I shall have to think twice about calling on her,' Grandma said to break the silence. Aunt Flora replied with a suitable, vague comment but Aunt Lallie was more brisk. 'It's said they're terribly wealthy, Mother – cotton. And by the way, I shall be going out this afternoon to see Beatrice.'

'You know that I don't approve of that friend of yours and her "Discussion Club" – her ideas are far too . . . modern.'

Jane felt Aunt Lallie was bottling up her feelings. Instead of saying, 'Mind your own business, I'll make my own decision thank you very much!' she compressed her lips and stared hard at her plate.

Cherry pie and 'Aunt Martha's brandy pudding'. Delicious, she would have thought normally, but Jane couldn't concentrate on food. Her mind was racing, thinking about the scraps of Uncle Dolly's angry argument she'd overheard and now this undercurrent of tension. What was going on? I don't want to know. I don't want to get involved. It's nothing to do with me.

'Jane! That's the second time you've been asked. Cherry pie or Aunt Martha's brandy pudding?' Grandma asked.

'Thanks,' Jane mumbled absently.

It was too wet for a walk in the afternoon. In front of the playroom fire, Lucy flicked over the pages of a heavy volume called *The Missionary's Daughter* while Henry pretended to be reading *Treasure Island*. He looked at his watch from time to time.

'It's "Good Reading" hour until three o'clock today as it's raining. We usually have it from five to six. We might have a few minutes to play with Wilf before tea if we can manage it,' Lucy said.

'That poor rat – it's no life for the poor thing, stuck in the back of your wardrobe.' Henry looked up from his book.

'But what could you do with it? If you gave it its freedom it couldn't fend for itself. It's too late – it wouldn't know how to get any food. The first cat to see it would pounce,' Jane said.

'Well, that's not going to happen – he's going to stay in his tin, safe and sound.'

Caged up, safe and sound . . . like Lucy herself, Jane suddenly thought . . . and like *she* was beginning to feel in her tight shoes and restrictive clothing. All hours of the day planned without any freedom or chance to do something unexpected or silly.

'Why do you keep looking at your watch, Henry?' Lucy asked.

'No reason.' Henry banged his book shut. 'Lucy . . .' he began.

'Mmm?'

But he didn't go on. He went over to the window and gazed out for a few moments, then left the room.

Jane couldn't immerse herself in *Bleak House* and didn't see why she should have to. The book was depressing too, about fog.

'I'm going down to the kitchen to have a chat with Jessie.' It might be more lively down there, she could hear about the Music Halls and hear some of the latest hits. 'Are you coming?'

'I'd better not.' Lucy replied.

It was Ivy's afternoon off and Jessie was just going to visit an aunt who was ill. Mrs Murphy was dozing by the fire, snoring.

'I won't be long. No getting into mischief now,' Jessie teased as she adjusted her bonnet in the small mirror by the back door and hummed the catchy tune from 'The Desert Rose' which Jane remembered being played on the barrel organ; she waved goodbye.

Up in the hall, Goff, the coachman, was struggling with a large wooden cabinet.

'What's that for? Can I give you a hand?' Jane asked.

'No, Miss, thanks all the same,' and he heaved it into the dining room.

'That's right, Goff, over here.' Uncle Dolly gestured to a suitable place and Goff let it slide from his hands on to the floor with a thud and wiped his brow.

'Why do you want a wardrobe in the dining room?' Jane asked, following them.

'To lock up inquisitive girls like you! Come and try it for size.'

Jane stepped inside, it wasn't the simple box that it seemed – it was painted black and there were mirrors inside. She caught sight of her reflection for a moment and again didn't recognise herself.

'For my new trick,' Uncle Dolly explained, rubbing his hands together. 'I'll get Henry to rehearse it with me.' And he turned his attention to the back of the cabinet.

An oppressive silence had fallen over the house. Jane went to see if there were any signs of life in the drawing room. Aunt Flora was gazing into space with her needlework on her lap. Dolly came in and took her hand, leading her to the dining room. Aunt Lallie had gone to see her friend, the unsuitable Beatrice, and hadn't returned yet.

Lucy came downstairs and joined them.

'Is your new trick going to be for the church concert?' Jane asked Uncle Dolly.

'Maybe and maybe not.'

'You must stay for it, Jane.' Lucy said.

'Maybe and maybe not.'

The sound of a brass band could be heard faintly in the distance.

'Oh dear,' Aunt Flora said, 'the Salvation Army. They're sure to disturb Mother while she's having her rest.' She went to sit on one of the dining room chairs, which Uncle Dolly had turned round to face the magic cabinet and Lucy and Jane went to sit on either side of her.

'Henry, there you are – where have you been? I need you to stand here,' and Uncle Dolly positioned him.

It's going to be like the trick when Lorna vanished at that party, Jane thought. Perhaps I'll be able to find out how it's done.

'Ladies and gentlemen. May I have a volunteer from the audience, who will be willing to disappear for three minutes?'

The noise of the band suddenly sounded much nearer. Cymbals crashed, tambourines were rattled and the steady beat of a drum kept up the tempo of the march 'Onward Christian Soldiers'. Some singing too.

'Marching as to war . . .' Boom! Clash!

'Thank you, kind sir,' Uncle Dolly had to shout now. 'Step this way, please.'

Henry was ushered into the cabinet. He turned and stared at Lucy. The door was closed and tapped in a theatrical manner with a wand. A loud chanting began with the now familiar words, 'Dolly, jolly, zambo!'

The band must have stopped right outside the house, Uncle Dolly shook his head in irritation. 'Bazooka!' he shouted and opened up the cabinet.

As Jane had guessed – no Henry to be seen. Lucy clutched at Aunt Flora in amazement and they clapped.

'Onward Christian Soldiers . . .'

The door was closed again. More tapping and chanting.

'Bazooka!' Looking at his audience, Uncle Dolly flung open the door with a flourish and waited for more applause – but none came. The cupboard was still bare. Uncle Dolly frowned, closed it up again and rapped more loudly and banged on it with his fist.

'Open Sesame!'

He wrenched it open but there was no sign of Henry. He poked about inside and strode round the back. No one there. Aunt Flora gave a shrill cry.

Jane sat on the edge of her chair and thought, Uncle Dolly really is a brilliant magician. But seeing his distraught face, she realised with a shock of horror that this was no trick – it had all gone terribly wrong.

Henry had gone.

Chapter 7

The music outside came to a stop after a violent rattling of tambourines and there was suddenly an eerie silence in the room. Then Uncle Dolly burst out angrily, 'The foolish boy is obviously playing some sort of jape.'

'But how?' Aunt Flora screamed and Lucy, catching her fright, started to cry.

'This is nonsense, he must be somewhere around – we'll have a search party,' Jane said.

'No . . . he's gone . . . You've put a fluence on him, Dolly. Haven't I always said "there are more things in Heaven and Earth than are dreamed of"? And what are we going to tell Mother?' Flora wailed.

'Oh, do be quiet, Flora. Jane's got the right idea. I shall go and look upstairs. You, Jane, go and search this floor.' He started shouting 'HENRY!'

'But we would have seen him if he'd left the room. He just disappeared into thin air . . . thin air,' Flora moaned. She and Lucy sat looking terrified. Jane realised they were right. It would have been impossible for him to have reached the dining room door without being seen.

Huddled together, Lucy and Aunt Flora left the room and

Jane was left alone. Was it possible that Henry was somehow squashed up inside the cabinet, unable to breathe, unable to cry out? She poked and prodded at the wooden and glass interior and discovered that the back swivelled to reveal an inner space, which in turn had a section which revolved, through which Henry could easily step out . . . but then what? It just meant that he would have been behind the cabinet and would have been discovered when Uncle Dolly had walked right round. The thick red dining room curtains reached the floor and hadn't been drawn although it was getting dark now, but it would have been impossible for him to have reached them without being seen.

She gazed round the room.

'Bazooka!' she said aloud.

Jane knew that, although well-concealed in the oak panelling, that funny curved knob if turned would open up to reveal the dumb waiter. Henry could easily have squeezed into that, just like I did, she thought. By pulling the rope, he would work the mechanism to carry him downstairs like a pile of food and stack of dishes and would arrive in the kitchen. Mrs Murphy is dead to the world – Ivy's got the afternoon off and Jessie has gone out so he could slip up the kitchen stairs and out of the back door without any trouble. Any noise would have been muffled by the Salvation Army band.

She went over to the dumb waiter and slid open the door. Peering down the shaft into the well, she could see that it had reached the bottom.

He was still missing though . . . and why? And where was he now? Why was he running away? It's none of my business, she reminded herself. I'm going home soon. Then she thought of Lucy's stricken face and decided to go down to the kitchen.

She went into the hall but met Aunt Lallie coming in through the front door. She was out of breath and flushed. With her hat on one side and hair blowing across her face, she looked wild; Jane noticed dark smudges on her cheek.

'This weather,' she said by way of explanation when she saw Jane and reached up to straighten her hat. They heard a soft tap tapping and the now familiar slight jangle of a chain of keys and, looking up in the gloom, saw Grandma slowly making her way downstairs with her walking stick.

'I'm coming down to see what all the commotion is about. Dolly shouting all over the place, Flora sobbing . . . Why can't I get any peace?' She reached the bottom of the stairs and, seeing her daughter, raised her stick as if to strike her but instead pointed at her head.

'What is the meaning of your disgraceful appearance? You look as if you've been in a common brawl!'

Lallie took off the offending hat and tried to straighten her dishevelled hair. 'Just the weather – a gale got up . . .'

'I don't hear any gale.'

Dolly suddenly came thumping down the stairs. 'Come into the drawing room, Mother. There's something you must know.' Lallie looked relieved to have the attention taken away from her. She removed her jacket and joined the others.

'I'll ring the bell for Jessie to bring tea,' Grandma said, settling herself in her usual armchair.

'I believe Jessie is visiting a sick relative – she'll be back shortly and never mind about tea for a moment . . . What I have to tell you is far more serious. Henry has gone missing – he has disappeared . . .'

'Don't talk nonsense, Dolly!'

'But it's true, Mother. Isn't it?' He turned beseeching eyes on the others to confirm his shocking story. They nodded.

'One of my tricks – the one with my new cabinet. Henry went inside and . . . never came out.'

'You're talking rubbish.'

Jane chipped in, 'But it is sort of true. He has gone but I think he escaped through the back of the cabinet, into the dumb waiter and down to the kitchen. I was just going to see if he was there.'

Not knowing whether to be relieved or upset, Uncle Dolly stormed out of the room shouting, 'I'll give him a piece of my mind, frightening us all like that!' Jane ran after him.

Mrs Murphy was just waking up but there was no sign of Henry. 'Have you lost something, sir?' she asked as they searched the larder, the butler's pantry and the scullery. The cellars were kept locked.

'No, no . . . perfectly all right, thank you, Mrs Murphy,' he lied before Jane could explain. Why didn't he tell her? Why didn't they phone Henry's friends – if he had any? He wasn't upstairs. Those rooms had already been searched.

'Well?' Grandma drew her lips together in a tight line. Uncle Dolly shook his head.

Lucy had gone upstairs but now came back into the drawing room. 'Father's army medals have gone. Henry always kept them by his bed and now they've gone.' She started to cry again softly. Jane put an arm round her. They all realised that the missing medals must mean that Henry's disappearance was premeditated, no random, spur of the moment joke.

'We must telephone the police,' said Jane decisively.

'The police! We will do no such thing!' Grandma said in

an icy voice, 'and not a word to the servants. As far as they are concerned, Henry is spending a night or two with a school friend. If he has not returned by tomorrow I may obtain the services of a private investigator.' She turned to Jane, 'And you, my girl, will not offer any uncalled for advice or we shall have to see about your returning home!'

'Mmmmm,' thought Jane, 'that might be quite a good idea.' How could they all just sit there? Why didn't they run out into the street, ask passers-by? It was getting dark now.

'Dolly, put a little more coal on the fire and ring for Jessie, the girl should be back by now. I don't pay her good money so that she can spend time visiting relatives. It's time the curtains were drawn and the lights lit. Flora, pass me that cushion.' And Grandma settled back comfortably.

Jane noticed an even stronger whiff of lavender than usual as Aunt Flora brushed against her. 'It wouldn't take a moment to phone a friend,' Jane muttered to her but 'Mother doesn't believe in those new-fangled instruments,' was all the reply she had from Flora, looking at her with piteous eyes.

After a short delay, Jessie arrived and on the surface, the late afternoon returned to normal but Aunt Flora's hand shook as she held her cup and saucer and Lucy gave one or two little shuddering sobs.

After tea had been cleared away, Grandma said, 'I think we'll have a game of whist. Get out the playing cards, Lallie. You can be my partner. Dolly – you can play with Lucy. Flora seems to be all fingers and thumbs today, she'd probably drop the whole pack whilst shuffling. Jane, I don't expect you know how to play, do you? I thought not. You can sit over there,' she pointed to a small table and chair near the door, 'and play patience.'

Jane was banished with her own pack of cards and the others, without any enthusiasm, began their game. The ornate clock of gothic design ticked loudly and chimed the hour. Uncle Dolly felt in his waistcoat pocket for his silver fob watch, forgetting for a moment that he'd taken it to be regulated. 'I must remember to collect my watch from Jessops tomorrow.'

Yes, you must, thought Jane. I need it. She looked at the cards unseeingly. There was no doubt that Grandma had been shaken by the letter which had been delivered last night. Did it have anything to do with Henry's disappearance? No, it couldn't have. And Uncle Dolly's message on that scrap of pink paper. What could Ivy, with her sharp face and cunning eyes, know about Uncle Dolly that was so secret?

The silence was suddenly broken by the loud jangling of the front door bell. Everyone froze.

'Perhaps it's Henry – I'll go and see,' and Jane got up and ran to open the drawing room door.

'Sit down.' Grandma's voice was furious.

Jessie's footsteps sounded across the hall, the front door was opened but it was a man's voice they heard, not Henry's.

'A gentleman's here, ma'am,' Jessie said.

'What name?' Grandma asked.

'Well . . . It's a policeman, ma'am.'

Jane thought quickly. Perhaps they've found Henry . . . Perhaps . . .

'. . . it's a policeman and it's Miss Lallie he wants to see.'

'Lallie?'

'It's all right, Mother. I'll see him.' And Lallie rose almost majestically despite her ruffled hair and unusually unkempt appearance. The door was left open and they all heard everything.

'Miss Lavinia Patterson?'

'Yes, that is my name.'

'I have reason to believe that you, together with some other ladies, were causing a breach of the peace this afternoon on Church Street, that you were affixing posters to a number of lamp posts, that a scuffle ensued and that a heavy object, namely a bottle, was hurled by yourself – through the window of a shop, by the name of Jessops, causing the said window to break. There were a number of witnesses present at the scene. Do you have anything to say?'

Uncle Dolly got up. 'This is outrageous,' he shouted. 'It's all a horrible mistake.'

But Aunt Lallie spoke out clearly, even proudly, 'No. What you say is perfectly true. I have nothing to say in my defence except that I did it for the cause and this is only the beginning. There will soon be a mighty army fighting for votes for women.' Her voice rose shrilly.

'This is some nonsense of that woman, Beatrice,' Grandma said to Dolly. 'I knew she was a bad influence on Lallie. Votes for women indeed. Whatever next?'

I've never thought about it, just taken it for granted. Votes for women. Where's the problem? Jane thought, amazed.

'So what happens now?' Lallie was shouting 'A prison sentence? Bread and water diet? I really don't mind. I'm only too happy to draw attention to our plight.'

'Aunt Lallie . . . going to prison?' Lucy whispered. Jane held her hand.

'Well, as it happens, you're in luck, Miss Patterson,' the

policeman said sternly. 'The proprietor of the shop is known to your family, I believe, and says he will not press charges in this instance on consideration of a sum of money to be given to repair the shop window. But you must take this as a very severe warning. Next time . . . Well, I trust there won't be a next time. But if there was, things would be very different – very different.'

'I don't care, I tell you.' Lallie was defiant.

'I'll be going then, Miss, but mark what I've said. We can't have ladies rampaging about the street, making a nuisance of themselves and causing a disturbance. Good evening to you.'

Jane had a sudden thought – we should mention Henry while he's here – quickly before he goes. 'Henry,' she shouted, 'we should tell him.' But the front door banged loudly and he was gone.

'Lallie. Come here.' Grandma's voice was frightening – not loud but low, soft, menacing.

Flora got up quickly, knocking the table and scattering the playing cards. 'I'm going to my room, Mother.' Dolly stood before the fire, looking down into the flames. Lallie came back in with her head held high.

'What is the meaning of this behaviour? You are a disgrace to your father's memory. He was respected by everyone in the neighbourhood. And as for that Beatrice! I forbid you ever to see her again. Do you hear me?'

'Yes, I hear you and now you listen to me. I have my own life to lead. I intend to have a prominent position in our campaign. We shall go from strength to strength. I shall go and stay with Beatrice – now – this very night. I shall just take a small case with me. I'll send for the rest of my things later.' She went to leave the room but turned for a moment. 'You must get Henry back.'

Jane took hold of Lucy's hand and they rushed out together, up the stairs, neither of them wishing to witness any more of the scene.

Lucy was shaking. Jane closed their bedroom door. 'Look,' she said but didn't know how to go on. Then she took her handkerchief from a pocket. 'I saved a few crumbs for Wilf.' She watched as Lucy went to feed her poor imprisoned rat and felt pity for her. She was lonely, her brother was missing and she'd shared her two sad little secrets with her – the locket and this small rat in the tin. This house was like a huge biscuit tin, she thought again, angrily, and Lucy was trapped inside. Jane felt an urgent need to get home, wherever it was, even to see Billa, with her off-hand manner, again.

After a quiet supper in the playroom, Jane suggested a visit to the stable loft to give Wilf some exercise. 'I don't think we'll be missed somehow,' she said.

They crept downstairs. No sound, apart from a slight rattle of plates, came from the dining room, where Grandma, Uncle Dolly and Aunt Flora ate in silence.

There was no proper lighting in the loft so Jane took a candle and matches from the kitchen windowsill while Mrs Murphy was shuffling around in the larder. They ran across the dark yard.

'I'll light the candle now,' Jane said at the bottom of the rickety stairs. Lucy went to soothe Bess, who had been startled by the sudden visitors.

The loft looked even more exotic by the flickering candle-light. Shadows played over the carved masks and shrunken heads (how could Mr Patterson have thought these beautiful?). The huge golden Buddha seemed to be looking at them through his half-closed lids.

'Here, Lucy, stick the candle on top of that gong, I'll manage Wilf,' and Jane took hold of the biscuit tin. Lucy grabbed at the candle and tried to place it on the gong but the surface was shiny, the candle slipped and fell on to the dry hay covering the wooden boards. In a second the hay had caught fire, flames spreading, devouring the hay hungrily with a terrifying crackling sound.

Lucy screamed and Jane dropped the tin, appalled. The whole place will go up in smoke, she thought with panic. We'll be roasted alive – we must do something – but what? She looked round desperately and saw the pile of old horse blankets. Seizing one quickly, she threw another at Lucy.

'Come on!' she shouted urgently. 'Beat the flames! Beat them!' To her horror, Lucy didn't move. She stood, still as a statue, frozen with terror.

'Come on! It's spreading.' Jane could already feel scorching heat. The fire had almost reached the wooden curios now, licking round them from all sides.

'Crush them, crush the flames!' Jane shrieked and taking Lucy by the shoulders, shook her violently. 'Think of poor Bess! If the floor gives way, it'll collapse on her. She'll be killed!'

The words shocked Lucy into action. 'No!' She took the blanket that Jane thrust at her and together they thrashed at the blazing hay.

'Keep going! I'm going to get some water.' And Jane, coughing and with streaming eyes, stumbled down the steps, found a bucket and filled it from the trough of water. She managed to lug it up to the loft without spilling too much, and then threw the water over the smouldering remains. There was a hiss and she ran back to fetch more water.

'That should do it.' She was exhausted after three trips with the heavy bucket and she and Lucy collapsed, panting on to the floor. 'Phew! We must look awful!' They looked at each other but could hardly see a thing in the dark.

'Wilf! The lid's come off the tin!'

Oh no, I don't believe this, Jane thought. They could just see the inside of the tin, which had fallen on its side in the dim light coming from the skylight. It was empty.

'Wilf's gone!' Lucy shrieked.

Their eyes were getting used to the dark now. 'We'll search – he can't be far,' Jane said but felt it would be a really hopeless task in this place with all the jumble, as she thought of it, stacked up.

'Move this junk.' They heaved pieces of wooden furniture and looked behind stacks of Oriental curios and delicate china. It was becoming even darker.

'It's no good,' Jane said.

'Don't say that – we mustn't give up.' Lucy sounded frantic. 'He must have been frightened by the fire.'

'Look, he's gone. We'll never find him tonight anyway.' Or any other night, Jane thought. 'He could have rushed down the stairs and be anywhere by now.' And she felt guilty as she'd been the one to drop the tin, but at least the rat was free – if he hadn't been attacked by a dog.

'He didn't want to be cooped up. I should think he was glad to escape. I'm sure he'll be happier.' But Lucy wouldn't be comforted. She seemed younger than her years and Jane put her arm round her. Poor Lucy, what a day. First her brother going off, then the police and her aunt storming off, and now this.

'Listen – we'd better get back or they'll think we've vanished too. Come on.' And she pulled Lucy, still reluctant, down the stairs and across the yard. They managed to creep through the hall and up the stairs without being seen. The gas light had been lit in their room and soon they heard Ivy, back from her afternoon off, coming along to supervise them. They'd hardly had time to dust themselves down and have a quick wash.

'What's that smell of smoke?' she demanded.

'The fire downstairs was smoking badly,' Jane said quickly, 'and we were sitting playing cards and . . .' but Ivy didn't seem very interested. She was in a chatty mood.

'Jessie tells me you had a visitor this evening.' She looked sly, malicious. 'A policeman, was it?'

Jane and Lucy didn't say anything. This 'keeping secrets', bottling things up is catching, Jane thought.

'Miss Lallie in a spot of trouble, I hear.' She brushed at Jane's hair almost viciously. 'Well, mum's the word, is it? And it's not the only thing I've heard either.' She suddenly began to sing, something that sounded vaguely familiar to Jane:

Daddy wouldn't buy me a bow wow
Bow wow.
Daddy wouldn't buy me a bow wow

'But I'll have enough to buy a cartload of bow wows soon, you'll see.' And she laughed.

'What's up with her?' Jane said when Ivy had gone.

'She was singing one of those cheap Music Hall songs that Grandma hates. Her young man, Arthur, takes her to some of the shows. He works backstage and she can get in without paying. Arthur is Sam's older brother.'

'Sam? You mean the boy who helps in the garden?'

'Yes, and he built Wilf's run in the loft.' Remembering Wilf, she started sniffing again.

'Wasn't Sam's father the one who stole the church silver?'

'Mmmm.'

Jane couldn't think how to cheer her up. It had been a traumatic day. 'Perhaps Sam can help you to find Wilf.'

'And where's Henry? What's happened to *him*?' Lucy cried.

'Can you think of anything that might give us a clue? Who were his friends? He may have gone to stay with one of them.' Oh, for a mobile! Jane thought.

'No – he wouldn't do that and he didn't really have any special friends – Grandma didn't encourage it.' Lucy thought for a moment. 'I've seen him talking to Sam once or twice, that's all.'

How could she have envied Lucy and Henry's life for a moment? Jane wondered. She was desperate to leave this prison – but she made a decision. 'Listen, I'll have to go home soon—'

'Oh no, don't leave me. I'll have no one.'

'I'll have to go home soon but I promise that I won't go until Henry is found.' What was she saying? How could she keep a promise like that? But Lucy seemed to have confidence in her.

'You will find him, I know, if you say you will. You're different.'

Yeah – I'm crazy, Jane thought.

The gas light flickered and went low. The room became darker. 'What's happening?' Jane asked.

'It sometimes does that when gas is turned up in another room,' Lucy explained. 'Anyway we'll have to put ours out now – it's time.'

They were meant to go to sleep as punctually as everything else happened in the house but Jane was still awake for some hours afterwards. She heard soft, padding footsteps seeming to come from the room above – the Tower Room. Perhaps, as Lucy said, when their gas light dimmed, another would grow brighter – in another room . . . in the Tower Room? Was someone up there?

Chapter 8

There was no sign of Henry next morning. And no sign of any agitation on Grandma's part, although Jane supposed she was about to contact a private investigator. On the surface, everything was calm but underneath, Jane thought, tempers and emotions were sizzling, bubbling, like a bottle of cola about to explode when the top is released.

Looking out of the window, Jane saw that a fog had come down. She could barely make out the laurel hedges in the front garden, then it cleared for a second.

'No going out today, Lucy,' Grandma said at breakfast, 'and Miss Norris will not be coming in this fog. Flora, you can supervise some French for the girls.'

Flora looked white and strained and jumped when Ivy banged down a coffee pot on the sideboard.

'I've got a meeting with the Waifs and Strays Committee this afternoon, Mother and it may run on a bit,' announced Dolly. 'I probably won't be in for dinner tonight.'

'You're spending far too much time on your committees, Dolly. Don't you think Flora and I would be glad of your company with Lallie and Henry away at the moment, staying with their friends?' This last remark was obviously for Ivy's benefit but Jane saw Ivy smirk knowingly.

'And by the way,' Dolly said, 'I'm going to send the boy, Sam, along to Jessops to collect my watch this morning – should be ready.' Jane saw Grandma give a slight start at the name Jessop and frown at Dolly.

Ivy gathered up some dishes with a clatter and started humming quietly, 'Daddy wouldn't buy me a bow wow' as she went out.

'Really, that girl! She'll have to go, Dolly. Your father wouldn't have put up with her in the house for one minute!'

Dolly looked uneasy and changed the subject suddenly. 'I can smell smoke, can you, Mother?' He sniffed the air.

Jane had just leaned over to pass the butter to Lucy, who was sitting next to Grandma.

'Yes, I can,' Grandma's thin, white hand reached out and grasped one of Jane's ringlets, 'and it is coming from here! What is the meaning of it?'

'Well, I sat too close to the fire last night when it was smoking and—'

'Rubbish, our fires never smoke. Lucy come here.' Lucy went reluctantly to her grandmother and had her hair sniffed.

'Hmmm – what has been going on? Answer me.'

Jane wanted to blurt out, 'It was this rat of Lucy's, it escaped in the stable loft in amongst all that crazy load of junk. The candle fell over and the place caught fire!' Why couldn't she tell the truth? But she knew she couldn't for Lucy's sake. She kept silent.

Grandma's eyes narrowed. 'I feel you, Jane, are becoming a bad influence on Lucy. I think it will be a very good idea if you return home first thing in the morning. I will tell Goff to have the carriage ready to take you and your . . . no, you didn't have any luggage, did you – back to your home.'

Lucy yelled out 'No!'

'You see, Dolly? You see what I mean . . . a thoroughly bad influence. Flora! Take them out of here.' She waved her arm imperiously and Flora, rising from the table, led the way out of the dining room.

Jane, dawdling as she went through the door, heard, 'Rusby's the name, sounds a reputable Agency from the advertisement in the *Echo*. That letter you received at the concert, Mother, do you think . . .' Dolly lowered his voice. She heard the name 'Muriel' then had to catch up with Aunt Flora, who was waiting for her.

There was no opportunity to try and keep her stupid promise to find Henry during the morning. Aunt Flora kept a watch on them in the drawing room. They heard the front door bang as Uncle Dolly went off on an errand. Goff was waiting for him with the carriage, barely visible in the patchy fog. Probably, thought Jane, off to the detective agency.

She saw Sam darting off down the road, presumably to collect the watch from Jessops, the jewellers. It was vital that she should get her hands on that watch, somehow. Her life – her proper life – depended on it.

'You're miles away, Jane. Get on with your French translation!' Even the rather feeble Aunt Flora had changed. Now there was a sharp edge to her voice. Her face looked parched and lined.

Jane was suddenly reminded of the rockery in the garden with the pretty stone embedded with pink sea shells and the maggots writhing away beneath. Take the lid off this house and you'd find all sorts of nasty things going on underneath.

The morning dragged by. Sam returned and, some time later, Uncle Dolly.

As they went in to lunch, Uncle Dolly looked upset. 'That fool of a boy came back empty-handed,' he said to his mother. 'Apparently my watch has gone missing after that . . . incident . . . at the shop yesterday.' Grandma frowned at him warningly – the servants might be listening.

This was terrible news to Jane. No watch meant she wouldn't be able to get back. She was as upset as Dolly.

'It can't be far,' she said. 'Why didn't Sam help them look for it?'

Grandma raised her eyebrows.

'Good of you to be concerned,' Uncle Dolly said. 'They did say they'll send someone round with it if and when it turns up.'

The visit to Rusby's wasn't discussed.

The day was passing and Jane felt Lucy's accusing eyes on her. She was far away from keeping that stupid promise she'd made to find Henry. When could she start?

'Well, I'm off to my Waifs and Strays meeting,' Dolly said when they'd finished pudding. He scraped his chair away from the table and heaved himself up.

'Goff can take you. This fog's getting worse,' Grandma said but Dolly put up his hand.

'No need, no need. The walk will do me good.'

'In this weather? And you know how you hate walking. Flora, tell Ivy to instruct Goff to—'

'No, I said.' He thumped his fist on the table.

'Thank you, Dolly, that will be enough,' Grandma said icily.

Aunt Flora ran from the room.

They're like a bunch of children, Jane thought.

The girls were meant to have a rest after lunch and Lucy flopped on to her bed miserably.

'I'm going out,' Jane told her.

'You've got an idea – about Henry?' She looked up hopefully.

'Sort of,' Jane lied. 'Tell them I've got a headache if I'm late for supper. Where's my coat? The one I arrived in.' She felt she might be glad of the warmth from Billa's fake fur out in the fog.

'It may be in a cupboard on the landing.'

It was and Jane was glad to see it. Snuggling into its furry comfort, which smelt slightly of a cheap scent Billa sometimes used, she felt more like herself. No one was about. She opened the front door quietly and stepped out.

Henry sometimes spoke to Sam, she remembered Lucy saying. She'd go and find him and see if he had anything to say.

It was not only foggy, it was freezing and she felt sorry for Sam when she found him at the back chopping wood, wearing a thin jacket much too large for his skinny frame. He looked up defensively and stopped his work.

'Well?' His eyes were hostile.

'Sam. Henry's gone missing.' Might as well come right out with it, never mind Grandma.

'So? What business is that of mine?'

'Well, Lucy says she's seen you chatting with him sometimes and I wondered if he'd ever said anything to you about going away – or anything,' she finished lamely.

He blew on his hands and rubbed them together. Steam rose from his breath. He was silent. Well, he had no reason to be helpful – probably felt he'd been marked down for what his father had done and been treated accordingly.

'Look, did he ever mention any place he liked . . . what did you talk about?'

'Ships.' He practically spat the word out. 'He'll have gone off on a ship . . . to foreign parts, far away.' He looked malicious now. 'Far away,' he repeated.

She hadn't expected this. It was a terrible idea and her heart sank. Of course, Liverpool was a port with huge ships coming in and out with cargoes.

'Banana boats an' cotton,' Sam was warming to his theme. 'Always looking for cabin boys. Foreign parts. Thinking about them myself . . . Africa, America . . .'

Or he could be a stowaway; Jane's mind raced ahead. They'd never find him, he could be gone forever. On the other hand, Sam might be talking wildly – leading her off a scent? She looked at him. His brother, Arthur, was Ivy's boyfriend. Had that been Ivy she'd overheard threatening Uncle Dolly? But he couldn't be all bad, surely? He'd made that run in the loft for Wilf. But maybe he just liked rats – was a bit of a rat himself.

They heard the front door bang. That would be Uncle Dolly going off for his meeting.

'Bazooka!' said Sam suddenly. 'He makes things disappear, don't he?' And went back to his wood chopping. 'Perhaps if he's so clever, he'll "Bazooka" him back!'

He knows something, I'm sure, Jane thought, pulling Billa's coat round her tightly. There was a tatty hood attached and she dragged it over her head for extra warmth.

Coming round to the front of the house, she could just make out the dark, plump shape of Uncle Dolly going down the path to the gate, carrying a case. Why hadn't he agreed to be taken by Goff? She darted behind a laurel bush in case he should turn round and see her. Why the suitcase? And suddenly she felt she knew.

Arthur and Ivy, perhaps with Sam's help, had kidnapped Henry. That message must have been a ransom note and the ransom was in the suitcase. They may get greedy and suddenly demand more and more. Henry might never be seen again. It was obvious Grandma knew none of this.

The gate clicked shut and he vanished into the fog. She'd heard about 'pea-soupers' and this must be one, like in a Sherlock Holmes film.

I must keep track of him. But what if he really is going to his old meeting? She pushed the thought aside. Just now, the problem was to keep Uncle Dolly in sight. Despite his build, he was a fast walker.

She followed him past all the other houses looming up like great ghostly galleons lost in a sea mist. Down roads empty apart from the occasional carriage and very occasional scurrying figure, muffled up against the bitter cold. Sounds were muffled, distant fog horns from the river kept up their depressing hoots, a steam train with its echo of a whistle in the railway cuttings, and the clock way up in the spire chiming the hour at St Enoch's.

After the church, she lost her bearings. Her eyes were watering with the acrid smell of the polluted air and she had to run now to keep up with the large black shape of Uncle Dolly, which kept disappearing in the blanket of fog.

I mustn't lose him, and anyway I'd be totally lost now if I tried to find my way back to The Laurels. Her fingers, as they pulled at her coat, felt pinched, her throat choky. Although still only the middle of the afternoon, gas lights had been lit and gleamed through the thick mist from time to time.

They seemed to be hurrying down a slope now – down towards the city perhaps? The street they were in was long and silent. She could hear her own quick footsteps and prayed Uncle Dolly wouldn't stop and turn round as she had to shadow him quite closely.

Then Jane heard someone walking behind her with a measured tread. Click, click, boots with heels. At that moment, Uncle Dolly suddenly stopped, shifted his case to his other hand, coughed and wrapped his muffler more firmly round his neck. Jane stood still, holding her breath and strangely, the footsteps behind came to a standstill. I'm being followed! No, I can't be – I'm imagining things. She glanced round, frightened but could only make out a dark shape, which might have been a tree. Why on earth should anyone want to follow me?

Uncle Dolly set off again. Jane hurried on, anxious not to lose him and again she could hear footsteps coming along behind purposefully.

They turned into another street with more gas lamps. A horse pulling its tram along tracks passed close by. A boy carrying a load of boxes nearly bumped into Jane and cursed loudly and she nearly lost sight of Uncle Dolly. Because this street seemed busier, she wasn't sure if she could still hear those distinctive footsteps. She was aware that the buildings were different. Grand houses had given way to more commercial premises. No front gardens and gates but some shops, ill lit or closed and, further on still, large terraces of blackened brick houses with smoking chimneys and steep steps leading up to shabby front doors; iron railings surrounding dingy basement areas. Then the fog, which had cleared briefly, came down again and it became more and more difficult to trail Uncle Dolly. There seemed to be pubs on every corner, lit up by gas lamps showing garish signs. A few men were lurching in the doorways shouting to each other. 'Hey, where's the fire then?' someone yelled at Jane as she barged through a small group.

She couldn't see what sort of large building it was that loomed up in a side lane and where Uncle Dolly finally came to a standstill. She stopped still herself and saw, through streaming eyes, a light over a sturdy door. He pushed at it and it opened with a great clatter and bang which seemed to echo in the narrow alleyway. Then he was gone.

If I follow him in right away, he'll see me and be furious. I'll wait a minute or two, she thought. There was no indication from the blank wall to show if it was an office block, the back of a chapel or anything else. It looked really uninteresting. She hopped up and down and shook her arms, trying to get warm, then she heard someone whistling: the tune grew louder and louder and a very tall thin man loomed into view, nearly knocking her over with a large case he was carrying.

'Oops!' He pushed open the door and she followed him in. It was a relief to be indoors again and to be able to see more than a few feet in front of her.

The man resumed his whistling and set off quickly with long strides down a corridor. Jane shadowed him cautiously, passing a door on which was pinned a large cardboard star and the words 'Little Daisy May'. For a moment Jane wondered if little Daisy May had anything to do with 'the Waifs and Strays' but then the door opened suddenly and a plump female emerged wearing a very full, short dress of red, white and blue, covered by a child's white pinafore and, on her head, a child's floppy sunbonnet. But she was no child, 'Daisy May'.

She's quite old, Jane thought . . . at least 39. Those gold ringlets are false. The dimpled face was heavily made up and a cigarette drooped between her crimson lips. She spotted the thin man, who was about to vanish round a corner and without removing the cigarette called out to him in a raucous voice, 'You're for it! Half an hour late. It's a shambles. He's in a right paddy, I can tell you!' But he just shrugged, waved his free arm and disappeared.

Her glittering eyes, almost concealed behind false eyelashes, came to rest on Jane.

'And 'oo are you, I'd like to know?' She looked her up and down, taking in Billa's scruffy coat and hood. ''Ere, look what the cat's dragged in, Nellie!'

Nellie, pale and pretty with her hands cupping a steaming mug, appeared behind Daisy May.

'Talking of cats – how would it do for you, instead of that moth-eaten bit of fur you have usually?' They both looked at Jane critically.

'Nah – too scrawny, too large,' was Daisy's verdict.

Jane pushed back her hood, she was shivering with cold and damp. 'What are you talking about? What is this place?'

Daisy May turned back into her room for a moment, stubbed out her cigarette on a filthy saucer and gave a loud laugh. '"What is this place? What is this place?" she asks. Well, ducks,' she put on a posh voice, 'This is The Old Duke Street Palace of Varieties don't you know. 'All the best in 'igh class h'entertainment.'

So, not a chapel then, Jane realised, but one of those cheap Music Halls so loathed by Grandma.

'And 'ere we are, in the middle of our dress rehearsal and only half the orchestra's turned up!'

'The kid looks half frozen, don't she, like one of them waifs? Come and have a mug of tea, ducks,' Nellie said, opening the door wider. The room behind looked cosy by gas light, full of brightly coloured costumes, some flung over a tall screen, posters on the walls, a comfy arm chair, bottles of beer and an old dressing table with the top covered in pots and jars and a mirror festooned with beads and feathers. It looked homely and Jane was tempted to stay awhile.

'Thanks, but I'm looking for someone.'

The sound of a jolly, rollicking tune could now be heard and Jane was drawn towards it as if pulled by a magnet.

'Who you wanting then?' Nellie called after her.

She turned briefly. 'Uncle Dolly.'

'Never 'eard of 'im.'

The brassy music grew louder – it sounded like a polka – one, two, three, hop! I used to do this at nursery, Jane thought and pranced round the corner and up some steps, where she stood stock still. A sudden bright burst of colour and the full blast of clamorous music bombarded her senses. She was standing amongst great flat boards of painted scenery, dangling ropes and edges of very long purple curtains. She nearly tripped over a red bucket containing sand.

On stage, against a background of a grand garden scene, complete with fountain, stately trees, classical pillars and flowerbeds painted in gaudy colours, four young, not very slim women were dancing a polka, kicking up their long skirts to reveal frilly petticoats underneath. Jane guessed this was supposed to be very daring. They were singing breathlessly and the orchestra was trying to keep up with their rhythm. Each time they landed heavily on the floorboards after a jump, a cloud of chalk – or was it dust? – flew up and one of the dancers started to cough.

'See me dance the polka!' Jane started singing along and wandered on to the stage. They were all lit up by an unnaturally bright white flare, coming up from the front. The coughing got worse, one of the dancers crashed into Jane and the music suddenly came to an abrupt and discordant stop.

Peering out with difficulty over the lights, Jane could see the conductor waving his arms frantically.

'Will someone tell me what is going on? Is this all part of the act?' He looked imploringly towards a small pulpit at the side of the stage, where a man with black curled moustaches and carrying a small hammer stood, rolling his eyes. 'Search me!'

The coughing stopped, Jane was pointed to some steps at the front of the stage, by one of the dancers and the music started up again.

It was dark off stage and Jane stumbled and almost fell on to the bench in the front row. No one took the slightest notice of her. She snuggled down and forgot why she'd come here.

The polka whirled to a frenzied finale and the man with the hammer shouted to an invisible audience, 'Show your devotion, ladies and gentlemen, to our delightful, delectable, divine, daring dancers, in the usual way by putting your hands together . . . and clapping!'

Jane, caught up in his enthusiasm, clapped loudly but stopped when she realised she was the only one.

'Dan de Lyon', debonair and droll, followed on with his comic capers to the accompaniment of his concertina, meant to be humorous and full of jokes that Jane didn't understand.

Then 'Archie Pelligo', introduced as the human penguin (piscatorial persona), waddled on to the stage. A shiny blue curtain was lowered over the garden scene to represent the frozen wastes and a tank of water on wheels pushed on by a struggling group of scene shifters, over which Archie, in full penguin costume, balanced on a tight rope and did a juggling act, wobbling precariously all the while. For his finale, he was handed a fishing net, fished around in the tank and produced wriggling fish of all sizes and colours, which he then held up and with his head thrown back, popped one by one into his mouth with apparent relish and swallowed.

'Uggh,' Jane said out loud.

There was a slight break for the tank to be removed and the blue curtain to be lifted.

One or two more members of the orchestra appeared.

'What sort of time d'you call this?' the conductor shouted at them furiously.

The tall, thin, whistling man was sitting just in front of Jane with his trombone. He turned and winked at Jane, who was still looking disgusted by the fish eaten alive. 'Just jelly,' he said, 'just jelly'.

The man with the small hammer waved it in the air and suddenly brought it down with a great bang. There was a dramatic drum roll and a loud crash of cymbals. 'And now, for your delectation, our star of the evening. We are privileged to welcome here, fresh from her triumph at the . . . at the . . . at the . . . Where was it, Charlie?' he shouted to the conductor, who shrugged his shoulders. No one seemed to know, and then Archie, now suffering from hiccups, popped his head round the side curtain and yelled, 'Wapping Empire.'

'At the Wapping Empire . . . the diminutive, devastatingly dimpled, dolcemente, darling of Dukes, dandies and daddies . . . our very own Little Daisy May!' Another bang of the hammer, drum roll and crash of cymbals and on walked the woman Jane had already seen, looking like a huge child, clutching a large furry toy cat under one arm and sucking at a lollipop. She cast an angry glance at the Master of Ceremonies for forgetting the scene of her triumph.

'Give us a smile, Daisy,' one of the orchestra shouted.

She tossed her fake curls and instantly went into her routine, smiling and simpering as the music started.

'Daddy wouldn't buy me a bow wow.
Bow wow.'

There was that song again. She ought to be looking for Uncle Dolly, Jane thought. One of the polka dancers came to sit next to her.

'All together now!' Daisy May encouraged her audience while stroking her cat.

'But I'd rather have a bow wow wow!' Jane and the woman sitting next to her did their best but the sound was rather thin.

Some bunting was lowered from above and, swapping her cat for a Union Jack flag, Daisy May next went into a rousing patriotic song, 'Red, white and blue', which involved marching and saluting a large picture of Queen Victoria held up by Archie, still giving the odd hiccup and Dan de Lyon, both disguised now as soldiers and looking very serious.

'The celebrity of her day,' Jane said out loud but her neighbour just sniffled. 'Off key,' she muttered.

The flag was thrown to one side and, with a flourish, Daisy May suddenly tore aside her skirt to reveal frilly pantaloons; a gaily painted bicycle was wheeled on to the stage. Jane could imagine the gasp this would produce when the actual show took place.

'Show off. Pity about those dreadful ankles,' the muttering went on.

'This is the song all my gentlemen friends sing to me and I'd like all of you out there to join in the last verse of this – my signature tune.' She pedalled round the stage, sedately, singing, 'Daisy, Daisy, give me your answer do' and trying not to notice the repetitive squeak of the cycle.

'But you'll look sweet
Upon the seat
Of a bicycle made for two.'

She finished with the word 'two' an octave higher and held the note as long as she could then jumped off her bike with a flourish and gave deep bows to centre, left and right.

There was obviously meant to be a storm of applause after this and Daisy May held her sweet 'little girl' smile for an instant then it was snapped off and she went to find someone to complain to, very loudly, about the squeak.

'What you doin' 'ere anyway, ducks?' her companion asked her as Jane half rose. Her eyes were becoming accustomed to the light now. The show was probably over and she'd wasted too much time. Uncle Dolly obviously wasn't here and she'd stupidly lost track of him altogether.

'Looking for Uncle Dolly,' she replied without much hope.

'Never 'eard of 'im. But you could ask Arthur, he seems to know everyone.'

'Arthur?'

'One of the stage hands, round the back.'

I know that name, Jane thought, Sam's brother, Ivy's boyfriend, whose father had pinched the silver. If I go and see him, perhaps . . . While she hesitated, there was yet another sharp tap of the hammer.

'Marvel now, ladies and gentlemen, at the mercurial, multifarious mystifications . . . the myriad, manifold manifestations,' the MC's voice rose to an almost hysterical pitch, '. . . the memorable, mesmeric, monumental magic of Merlin the Magnificent Magnifico.' A loud drum roll.

'What's he on about?' Jane paused then sat down again quickly as there was an explosion of light blue smoke. A trap door opened from the stage floor and up shot a figure in a dark blue cloak covered in stars and moons. He had a black beard, a pointed hat and a frightening face – dead white, fierce black eyebrows drawn together in a frown over blue mascaraed eyes. He tapped his wide sleeves with a wand and shook them, showing them to be empty. Then he shook them again and cried out, 'Dolly, jolly, zambo!'

Uncle Dolly!

Chapter 9

Uncle Dolly's secret was revealed – his other life as a Music Hall entertainer – and knowing this, Ivy and Arthur had a hold over him.

He went through an astonishing repertoire, using his familiar patter, waving white gloved hands.

'Hey presto!'

'Before your very eyes!'

'Now you see it, now you don't!'

'Bazooka!'

At the last bazooka, he took off his magician's hat and there, underneath it, was a white rat! Wilf!

It was the end of his act. Jane rushed up the steps through the wings and back on to the stage. She was afraid Uncle Dolly might do a vanishing act and disappear himself. He had his back turned to her.

'Uncle Dolly!'

He swung round and didn't seem to recognise Jane at first. The matt white make-up on his face had little streams of sweat running down it and the eye make-up was smudged. He was Merlin now and not Adolphus Patterson.

'It's me, Jane. I followed you . . . I thought . . . I . . .' she gabbled.

He didn't look pleased to see her. 'So you know my little secret now, do you?'

The band was packing up, everyone was leaving. The rehearsal was over; soon the place would be empty.

'You know my secret,' he repeated. 'You, Ivy, Arthur . . .'

'I won't tell anyone, I promise. Anyway, you must have much more fun here than you do at home.'

He didn't take any notice of her words. 'It won't make any difference after tonight. I'm going to make a clean breast of it and go right away to London. I've got good contacts at the Hippodrome. In the meantime—' He put his face close to hers. He looked sinister, his dark eyes furious, 'no one's going to tell tales on Uncle Dolly before he's ready.' He reached forward to grab her.

'There's a little place I know where you'll be quite safe for a few hours. The evening performance finishes at ten o'clock. I'll release you then. We can return to The Laurels together.'

'Grandma will send someone to look for me at tea-time,' said Jane.

'I think not,' he replied chillingly. They thought they were there on their own but there was a sudden sound off stage. Daisy May complaining about the squeaky bicycle and Uncle Dolly put his hand over Jane's mouth. 'We won't have any yelling, thank you.' She made a quick lunge but was gripped by steely fingers. She suddenly spied, looking out of a pocket in the black cape, Wilf's twitching nose.

'Ah, you've spotted Lucy's rat. Goff found him in the stable – very careless of her to lose him, so he's back in the act. You may borrow him for company.' And he propelled her across to the other side of the stage, through a door and pulled her down a steep flight of steps. It was dark. She could speak now.

'Where's Henry? I thought . . .'

'What has Henry got to do with anything?'

So, she'd been on a wild goose chase. He didn't know any more about the disappearance than she did nor did he sound concerned. He was just interested in his own problems. Had he even been to the private investigator that morning?

He took the rat out of his pocket and pressed it on Jane: while it struggled, he quickly strode to the door, went through and locked it behind him.

There was no window but a very faint light came from up above. No sound, people would have gone to their dressing rooms, be having something to eat, perfecting their acts for tonight. She had no idea of the time. She sat down on an upturned box.

'Poor Wilf.' She tried to calm him, stroking his fur, and they both shivered in the dark chill of the basement. Then Jane heard a sound, a squeak and then another one and then another, coming from overhead. Daisy May's bicycle. We're right under the stage. It sounded as if she was trying out her bike but it hadn't been fixed satisfactorily and the star's voice could be heard raised in anger.

I must get out of here, she thought and started to yell. A member of the orchestra decided to run over his score of 'Daisy, Daisy' and Jane's shouts were lost in the notes of the trombone.

Her eyes were getting used to the darkness. The place was full of boxes and tins of paint. She stood up and walked round, popping Wilf into her pocket and holding him there.

On the floor nearby a square had been marked out in white. She stepped onto it wondering what it meant – nothing probably. At that moment Wilf decided to make a bid for freedom clawing and scrabbling desperately, taking Jane by surprise. 'Keep still, there's a good rat.' Trying to keep her balance with her other hand, she reached out and discovered a metal lever. It felt strong and she grabbed at it. It shot forward. 'Whoosh.'

She and Wilf were whizzed up through the air in a manic ascent. Steel petals, like those of a giant flower, opened above her and they were spat out on to the stage to the shock and amazement of Daisy May, who fell off her bicycle and cursed loudly.

'You!' Her eyes were blazing.

Jane was just as shocked. Uncle Dolly's secret 'puff of smoke' entrance revealed.

'Sorry. Really sorry,' Jane shouted but she was so relieved to be freed, she didn't stop to help and fled through the wings, down the corridor and found the heavy door with its iron bar which she pushed hard and they were out. Out in the fog again, which hadn't lifted.

Wilf seemed subdued now after the fright and had settled down in the depths of her pocket.

It's perishing! Jane pulled the coat round her again and took what she hoped was the right direction. If I keep going uphill . . . She passed one of the pubs and turned the corner. It was very quiet here and dark now. Now and again she could just make out cracks in the curtains of a few houses, where lamps had been lit and wished she was safely indoors too.

It was so quiet that her own footsteps sounded quite loud

on the pavement. Her own footsteps and . . . there were some others she could hear too. Tip, tap, tip, tap.

Oh no, not again!

Shouldn't there be another pub on the right? I'm sure there was. She began to quicken her pace until she was almost running. To her terror the footsteps behind echoed more loudly now and were hurrying too.

I'm lost and I can't go on. She was out of breath, sobbing, had a stitch and had to stop. Bent double against a wall, she waited, petrified as the horrible 'click clack' drew near and came to a halt. She felt a hand on her shoulder and tried to scream but was too shocked to make a sound. Why should anyone have been following her like that? Why? Who was it? Terrified, she turned round and saw the figure in black she'd seen before from the window and by the church, veiled so she couldn't see the face.

'Who are you – why are you following me?' Jane found her voice but it sounded very weak.

'Don't be frightened.' The voice was low, a woman's voice. 'Lucy, don't be afraid.' She put her black gloved hands round Jane and drew her up.

'You're making a big mistake.'

'I've seen you looking out of the window. You must know me, darling, you must.' The woman sounded frantic. She lifted her veil. The face beneath was pale and tired looking but Jane suddenly remembered seeing the sweet expression in those eyes before, somewhere. Where? The locket, the picture of Lucy's mother . . . long gone. Was this an awful apparition?

'I'm not a ghost, Lucy. I'm real. I'm your mother. Did they tell you I was dead? So cruel, so cruel.'

'But I'm not Lucy.'

She looked stunned and put a hand to her throat. 'Where is Lucy? She's all right, isn't she?'

'Yes, she's all right. She's very unhappy.' If she was Lucy's mother, she was Henry's too. 'Henry's gone.'

She didn't seem disturbed by this news. 'Henry's safe,' she said softly, 'he saw me by the house once. I went up to speak to him but someone came out of the gate. When he went back for his prayer book on Sunday, I was there and was able to talk to him this time. We arranged to meet.' The two stood there, damp and cold in the fog, looking at each other.

'There's a tram shelter round the next corner – we can talk for a minute or two,' Lucy's mother said and put her arm round Jane.

Lucy's mother! This is incredible, Jane thought. How could she have been missing for all those years? How could she be alive and not contact her children? She seemed to know this area. There was the tram shelter. They sat down.

'And who are you?' The woman asked curiously.

Difficult to explain.

'They think I'm Grace but I'm really Jane.'

'Well, I know you're not Grace – she's with her mother, Muriel, and that's where I've been staying since . . .' she paused.

That must be 'poor Muriel', Jane thought, and said, 'She was meant to come and stay at The Laurels – I arrived instead.'

'Her visit was put off. Surely they got the message . . . it must have gone astray, I suppose . . . and you say you arrived instead.' But fortunately she didn't sound really interested in Jane's sudden appearance at The Laurels.

'I saw you following Dolly. Henry told me Lucy usually

goes to piano lessons on a Monday afternoon with a Miss Norris and I thought I must pretend Lucy had dropped a letter and give it to her in the hope that she would read what I had written. Not a very clever idea but I was desperate. Then you came along – by yourself – such a lucky chance. You moved so fast and when you stopped for a second, Dolly was near you, wasn't he? And I couldn't let him, or any of the family see me. They'd somehow stop me getting my children back.' A frightened look passed over her delicate face.

'But I don't understand how you could have gone away and left them for so long. How could you?'

'Do you think I wanted to?' she asked almost savagely. 'That wicked woman had me taken away to the Institution – the Asylum – and there I have remained with only dear Muriel keeping in touch with me until last week when I was discharged, being now restored to full health and of sound mind.' She spoke these last words bitterly. 'No one believed me, you see . . .' she trailed off, then continued in a more brisk tone. 'A letter was sent to The Laurels, I know, from Dr Passmore and I have been staying with Muriel.'

Jane remembered the letter arriving at the soirée, which had almost shaken Grandma's composure.

'Muriel has family in Canada who are willing to welcome me and the children into their home – a new life, a new start for us all, very soon. And you must help me now, Jane.' She squeezed Jane's hands.

'What can I do?' Jane looked into the other's eyes and believed her wretched story. She could hardly imagine how Lucy would take it all in when she knew the truth. 'What can I do to help?'

'Henry and I will come tonight at half past ten to The

Laurels and will wait outside. You must explain to Lucy and bring her downstairs and out by the back door. There should be no one about then, it should be quiet. You will do this for us, won't you? You must be her only friend.'

'Well, almost.' Jane drew Wilf, who was getting restless, out of her pocket. 'She has this pet, Wilf – it used to be in one of Uncle Dolly's magic tricks.'

'Poor Dolly – a sad man. He wanted to go on the stage but of course, she wouldn't hear of it.' She stroked Wilf's head and smiled, suddenly looking younger, prettier.

'Lucy and I will be at the back door at ten thirty, you can count on it,' Jane promised.

They walked hand in hand back to the house, their footsteps echoing in the damp, silent roads. Just before they reached the gate, Lucy's mother stopped. 'I can never thank you enough. Be sure no one sees you. They wouldn't let her go.'

'We'll be really careful, I promise.' Jane suddenly thought of something. 'You said earlier . . . What wouldn't anyone believe?'

'She knew the truth but wouldn't let anyone believe me.'

This doesn't really answer my question, Jane thought. She opened the gate stealthily. Lucy's mother started to disappear into the fog. Her voice came back faintly, 'The Tower Room . . .'

As she crept through the unlocked back door and along the passage by the kitchen, Jane could hear Mrs Murphy grumbling about something to Jessie, then she heard Sam's voice.

What was he doing here? Surely he should have gone home by now.

She edged her way along, through the hall, just the sound of the clock ticking, and up the dark stairs – no sounds at all.

Where would Lucy be at this time of the day? Then Jessie suddenly came out into the hall and rang the gong. The noise echoed upwards. Time for the evening meal and Jane could hear Lucy coming along the landing. She and Aunt Flora went down stairs.

Quickly she took off her coat, wringing wet now, strands of fur clumped together.

'Is that you Jane? I thought you were lying down with a headache.' This was Aunt Flora.

'Yes, I just wanted to get a drink of milk from the kitchen,' she lied.

'Well, come down quickly or you'll be late for dinner.'

'I'll just go and wash my hands.' Lucky, thought Jane, that she can't see what a real mess I look.

No chance to say anything to Lucy. Over the banisters she could just make out her white face and questioning look. She quickly popped Wilf into his old biscuit tin still in the wardrobe.

Dinner was a subdued affair with the depleted numbers – no Aunt Lallie now, no Henry, no Dolly.

'These Waifs and Strays meetings that Dolly has to attend go on far too late,' Grandma said to Aunt Flora. 'And I hope you realise that you girls are only staying up for dinner tonight to give your aunt and me some company and conversation. Have you packed your . . . your' (she couldn't bring herself to describe the jeans and T-shirt Jane had arrived in as 'clothes') 'your things, Jane, as you will be returning home tomorrow?'

She would be returning tomorrow. She's absolutely right, Jane thought. She longed to say something to Lucy, to shout out all the things she'd learned. 'Listen, everyone! Henry's safe. He's with his mother and Lucy will be as well, very soon. As for Uncle Dolly, he's in a Music Hall act, going to make it his career, off to London.' But she had to sit there stiffly, in damp boots, sipping chicken broth from a silver spoon and talking about church embroidery.

She tried to give Lucy a reassuring smile.

'It's no laughing matter.' Grandma rounded on Jane, catching the expression on her face. 'Really, a few days here don't seem to have done you any good at all. Your hair! Your fingernails! I don't know what poor Muriel is thinking of!'

Poor Muriel? Kind Muriel, helpful Muriel, brilliant Muriel, I'd call her and I'm sorry that I'll never meet her . . . or Grace, thought Jane.

If Grandma was desperately worried about Henry, she didn't show it. She sat upright and stony-faced, relying on Dolly and the private investigator to sort things out.

'A game of cards this evening, I think – the four of us,' Grandma pronounced. This change in routine, letting Lucy stay up beyond her usual bed-time, was the only sign of some inner disturbance, things gone wrong.

The clock in the drawing room ticked away. Sam shuffled in with a load of logs for the fire.

'Be careful, boy! You're leaving a trail of wet leaves behind you,' Grandma said furiously.

There was just one leaf. Sam banged down the logs in the

hearth, picked up the leaf and flicked it disdainfully into the fire, giving her a look of hatred before he left the room.

'I think I shall go to bed now, Mother,' Aunt Flora said, yawning. 'I feel one of my migraines coming on.'

Lucy and Jane started to yawn, Jane's yawn sounded more like a loud groan, long drawn out, carrying all the pent-up emotion of the evening.

'Hand over your mouth!' rasped Grandma. 'You two had better go up now too. I may see you in the morning before you go but it is unlikely. Flora will see you off the premises,' she told Jane. As if I'm a speck of dust to be brushed away and forgotten about. She and Lucy got up and Lucy gave her grandmother a brief kiss goodnight. This may be the last time you see her, Jane thought.

They followed Aunt Flora up the stairs as the grandfather clock struck ten and said goodnight to her, then escaped to their bedroom.

Jane closed the door behind them, almost exploding now. Lucy looked at her.

'Did you have any luck? Have you any news . . . Henry?' her voice faltered, she tried to brace herself for disappointment.

'News? News? How's this for a start?' And Jane flung open the wardrobe door, plonked the biscuit tin on Lucy's bed and opened it.

The rat, suddenly jerked out of his sleep after an exciting day, sat up, his nose twitching. Lucy grabbed at him and smiled as though her small mouth would split, 'Wilf!' she shrieked.

'Shhh. We'd better not make too much noise. If someone

comes here . . . We're going to be busy. Listen – sit down – I've some totally amazing news for you.'

Lucy caught the serious note in Jane's voice. She sat down on the bed. 'Henry?'

'Henry's safe. He's with . . . with your mother.'

Lucy looked uncomprehending and then shocked. 'What do you mean? He can't be. My mother . . . my mother . . .'

'Lucy,' Jane said gently, 'your mother is alive and well. Henry is with her and you will be too very soon. She's missed you so much all these years. There's been some terrible mistake.' Jane tried to choose her words carefully, better not to say too much. Her mother could explain in her own way, later on. 'It's really true – she's pretty, just like the picture in your locket.'

'If it's honestly true, where is she? Why isn't she here, now?' She was starting to get hysterical with shock and excitement. She clung to Wilf, who scrabbled desperately. 'You're making it up.'

'Calm down. I promise you, I'm not. It's going to be wonderful for you. We've got to hurry.' Jane explained briefly about the meeting with her mother and why it had to be a secret, although she didn't fully understand everything herself.

Lucy was quiet now. Then she said, 'You are speaking the truth, aren't you?'

Jane nodded. 'Yes, of course I am. Now, put a few of your special things into this pillowcase. I'll help you. The back door at half past ten, we must hurry.' Lucy seemed in a daze as she dropped in one or two favourite books, her locket, a dress. 'Can't you come too?' she asked Jane.

'I have to go . . . home. I'm not really Grace – just a friend. I have to go home.'

'I still want you to come.'

'You'll be fine, honestly.' Jane had found her own clothes bundled up in the cupboard on the landing. She put on her jeans, T-shirt and trainers and remembered the gaudy plastic hair slide she'd popped into her pocket. She held it out to Lucy. 'Here – a keepsake. It's for your hair.' She hadn't anything else.

'It's lovely, it's different. What can I give you?' Lucy looked at the biscuit tin. 'Take Wilf.'

Jane knew what it meant, the thought of giving up her greatest treasure.

'That's great of you, thank you so much but I can't take Wilf where I'm going.'

Lucy looked relieved. 'I'd better go and say goodbye to Grandma.'

'Not this time.' There were so many things that would have to be explained to Lucy, more shocks and surprises. She would suddenly grow up but her mother would tell her everything in her own good time.

'Come on, we'd better be going.'

Carrying the pillowcase and the tin containing Wilf they crept towards the head of the stairs, pressed up against the wall. Despite a thick coat, woollen scarf and velvet beret, Lucy shivered, her teeth were chattering. There was a dim light in the hall below. One of the stairs creaked as they started to descend and they stopped for a second, frightened that someone might hear.

Then suddenly, the brooding silence of the house was shattered. They heard the front door crash open, stomping footsteps on the polished floor and singing, very loud, echoing through the lofty hall. It was a man's voice.

'Two lovely black eyes, Oh, what a surprise . . .' It sounded somehow triumphant.

Then a door opened. The girls froze. It was the drawing room door. Grandma hadn't gone up to bed.

'Is that you, Dolly?'

The singing grew louder.

'Have you been drinking?'

'Only for telling a man he was wrong . . . Two lovely black . . . eyes.' He finished on a defiant note. 'Maybe I have, maybe I haven't, Mother.'

Jane had completely forgotten that Uncle Dolly would be returning after the show. He must have noticed that she'd escaped from under the stage when he'd gone to use the trap door for his act. Had he been worried? He sounded as if he was past caring about anything.

'And what I do is my own concern from now on. Do you understand?' There was great bitterness in his voice.

'Let us have no more of this nonsense, Dolly and please keep your voice down. You'll not only wake up Lucy and Jane but your sister and the staff.'

'Jane?'

Jane liked to think she detected a note of relief in his voice that she'd somehow made her way home.

'Come into the drawing room, Dolly and we can discuss this quietly.' She was cajoling but it was no good.

'I've come to say goodbye, Mother.' He burst out, 'The Music Hall is the life for me! You've always known my ambition, haven't you? But you've thwarted me at every turn. Now I'm going to live the life I've always wanted and there's not a thing you can do about it.'

Peering now through the banisters, Jane could see him

bring his fist down heavily on a small table covered in ornaments, which rattled under the thump.

'I packed a bag earlier,' he said in a quieter tone and retrieved it from the cloakroom. 'I've left one of my boxes somewhere . . . but no matter . . .'

Grandma made no sound.

More loud footsteps, the front door slammed and he was gone.

Jane was aware of slight scurrying noises and doors being very quietly shut in other parts of the house before it became silent once more. Then the clock in the hall struck the half hour. Jane and Lucy looked at each other, horrified. Half past ten. Lucy's mother and Henry would be waiting, for how long? Would they think she wasn't coming, didn't want to come, had been stopped by Grandma?

They heard the door of the drawing room open. Jane saw by the hall light the figure of Grandma go through and the door closed behind her.

'Now, quickly!' She took Lucy's hand and the two of them raced down the stairs, through the hall, through the passage to the kitchen area and to the heavy, back door. By a faint light coming from the half-closed door of the kitchen, Jane could just make out a large key, which she turned, and two iron bolts which she pulled back with trembling hands.

Lucy's own hands were damp with excitement now. 'I can't turn the knob!' Together they twisted it round and heaved. The door flew open. It was very dark but they could see a small light a little distance away, which came nearer. Henry was carrying a small, portable oil lantern and by his side was his and Lucy's mother, with her arms outstretched.

There were hugs, tears, no time for talk.

'We must go quickly – there is a carriage waiting for us at the end of the road.' They turned to Jane, who had stayed hesitantly by the door.

'How can I thank you? I can tell you've been a real friend to my daughter,' and Lucy's mother gave her a quick hug. 'Grandmother will find out what has become of Henry and Lucy soon enough. Muriel's lawyers will write and tell her as soon as we're safely away,' she said quietly, and then added fiercely, 'I can never forgive her for what she did to me. I spoke only the truth.' Then, gathering Lucy under the shelter of her cloak, they said goodbye.

Lucy turned for a second from the comfort of the cloak. Jane could see the white face in the black folds.

'Write to me. Write to me, Jane, promise.'

'I promise,' Jane had to lie. Through tears she saw the three move off, then vanish into the darkness.

What sort of a life would Lucy be going to? Jane wondered. More normal and more loving than the one she'd been leading, she was sure.

She slipped back through the door and turned to lock it and draw the bolts back into place. Her one thought now, to get back to Billa. One of the bolts was stuck and while she was tugging at it, she heard a low unpleasant laugh.

Chapter 10

Terrified, she clung to the bolt and thought of opening the door again and running out into the dark.

'So, Miss Lucy's done a runner 'as she? Same as 'er brother, same as 'er Uncle . . . and same as 'er aunt – won't be no one left 'ere soon, will there? All bazookered away.'

She turned round to see Sam standing in the kitchen doorway, silhouetted by the light of a flickering fire. She'd forgotten he was spending the night here because of the fog. How much had he heard? How much did it matter now? His brother Arthur and Ivy knew all about Uncle Dolly's double life but Uncle Dolly had gone right away now, beyond the reach of blackmail.

'Yes, Lucy and Henry have gone and I'll be off too in a minute.' She doubted he would say anything of this to Grandma, knowing how he hated her.

'Just as well, I should say. The sooner you've gone the better. They're all crazy in this 'ouse.' Then his voice softened unexpectedly. 'You can't go out like that – you'll freeze to death.' He looked at her curiously. No wonder, she must look strange in her jeans and T-shirt. And it reminded her of something – Billa's coat! She'd be in big trouble if anything happened to that.

'Thanks,' she said, 'you're right.'

She dashed quietly up the stairs two at a time and into the room she'd shared with Lucy.

The gas light was flickering and as she went to pick up the damp, bedraggled coat from the bed, the light started to dim. Lower and lower it went as if an invisible hand was turning down the jet. Then it went out altogether and she stumbled and fell. She remembered Lucy saying that if the light dimmed in one room, it flared more brightly in another.

She reached out for the coat in the dark and as her fingers touched the wet fur, she froze. A sound was coming from up above . . . the sound of sobbing, the same sound that she'd heard on her first night in the house. It was coming from the Tower Room. Someone was up there, someone who'd turned up the gas jet and was making those wailing, piteous cries. Someone . . . or something.

The Tower Room . . . She knew the truth. Lucy's mother had said those words. Some secret was connected to that room. I must know what it is – I must know, Jane thought. Before I go, I'm going to find out. I can't leave here now without knowing. Pulling the coat round her, she found her way to the door. Slowly, she climbed the steep stairs and stopped at the top. There was more moaning, louder now. Jane felt for the knob of the door to the Tower Room. Quietly, don't make a sound, she told herself, turning it round.

She tried twice but it was useless. It was locked.

What could she do?

She thought of the little stone balcony with its iron railings outside her bedroom window. Would Sam have a ladder?

Downstairs again, she knocked softly at the half-open kitchen door. Sam had been dozing in a rocking chair before the embers of the fire and jumped up, startled. 'What is it?'

'I need help! There's something up in the Tower Room.' She suddenly remembered that he'd made that run in the stable loft for Wilf. Perhaps he was an animal lover. 'It may be a trapped animal. The door's locked and we may need a ladder.'

'To climb up the outside? I'm no window cleaner. You're crazy, like the rest of 'em.'

'No, there's a little balcony outside my room. We might reach it that way.'

'Well, I'll 'ave a look,' he said grudgingly and yawned. 'Look, I don't want the old lady catching me – she's a holy terror.'

'She's in the drawing room. We'll have to be really quiet.'

They crept upstairs and pulled open the sash window of the bedroom. The light from the gas lamp had strangely become a little brighter and there was now no sound from above.

Icy, dank air came into the room as they climbed out on to the narrow balcony, which was surrounded by a decorative, spiky iron railing.

Jane looked up. 'There's a light there – in the room.' But Sam was looking at the forbidding walls of the exterior, wondering if it was possible to scale them.

'It's no good is it?'

'You might be in luck.' They both spoke at the same time.

'Look at this.' Sam slapped some stonework by his side and Jane saw solid steps leading upwards, helping to support the roof. They were very steep, with narrow stone treads, not meant to be climbed but necessary to the structure.

'We can't climb up those. Far too risky . . . Isn't it?' Do I really want to do this? Jane thought. The steps looked green and slippery and led up to the roof.

'Easy. I'll go first.' Sam was already testing the first tread, the heel of his boot hanging over the edge. 'Come on. I'll turn round and give you a hand up.'

Jane looked behind her. It was a very long way down. If they fell, the narrow balcony would do nothing to break their fall.

'Don't look down!'

I am mad. I should have gone straight to the dumb waiter and . . . But Sam was on the second step now, holding out his hand, so she looked up instead and felt herself being hauled up gradually by a strong grip. Her trainers scrabbling against the hard stone, she reached the top. In turn, they grasped the top of the parapet and pulled themselves over into the lead-lined gutter and cautiously made their way along towards the nearest window of the Tower Room.

They looked in. Their view was obstructed by a large folding screen.

Sam shrugged his shoulders. 'Now what?' he asked in a hoarse whisper.

'We've got to get in.'

There was a sash window facing her – one of three and it looked as if it hadn't been shut properly. She tried to push it up but it was stiff and took their combined effort to move it. It went up with a clatter. Suddenly the light in the room was dimmed and Jane hesitated.

'Come on, you can go first, I'll shove you up,' Sam said.

'Thanks a lot,' she replied, but he didn't seem to notice the sarcasm in her voice and steadied her as she climbed through the window. The large screen blocked any view of the room.

There was not a sound other than the faint hissing from the gas. Sam joined her and they stood, silent, for a moment. Then Jane, holding her breath, looked behind the screen. In the semi darkness she saw the octagonal shaped room, lined by dark wooden cupboards. Shelves, high up, held china and glass ornaments. There were paintings on the walls of varying sizes – some of which looked familiar to her. Some gin and whisky bottles lay on the floor.

The silence was more frightening than any noise.

The floorboards were bare but in front of one of the cupboards, which was partly open, there lay a crumpled black heap.

Was it just an empty store room?

Suddenly, behind her, Sam sneezed. Jane watched in horror as, without warning, the dark mound shook and rose up with a terrible cry.

Jane shrank back against Sam and the two of them fell, bringing down the screen with a resounding crash. Loud sobbing now came from the figure in front of them and wild cries of, 'No, you mustn't, you mustn't!'

It was human – it sounded like a woman – a demented one, Jane thought, standing up and making a move towards her.

'Don't, don't come any nearer. Nobody must see . . . Nobody!'

With a sickening realisation, Jane knew who it was: Aunt Flora. Aunt Flora with wild eyes, her long hair loose from its pins, hands shaking violently, while she tried to pull her black shawl round her shoulders.

Moved to pity, Jane went towards her. 'What is it, Aunt Flora? What's the matter?'

'I've told nobody. Lallie's gone . . . and Dolly . . . Henry and . . . It's too much . . . they'll find out,' she rambled on and started to moan loudly.

Jane looked at Sam, who was right behind her. He said, 'I told you. They're all off—' but before he could finish, they heard another noise. It was a tap, tapping and coming nearer. Then silence.

Flora turned petrified eyes towards the door. They all stood stock still. Very, very slowly the knob of the door was turning. It stopped then turned the other way. They all watched as if hypnotised. Then they heard a key being placed in the lock and turned, then once more, the knob was tried.

Little by little, the door started to open with a soft creak.

Aunt Flora cried out as a dark shadow, like an avenging angel, appeared on the opposite wall, large, menacing. Then they heard a familiar voice, cold with fury.

'The key, Flora. Where did you get the key?' Grandma rapped her stick on the floor. 'Answer me at once.'

'That time the tank burst . . . the flooding. You were away with the Bishop's sister, you didn't know. I took your key from the chain in your desk. Workmen came.'

'You put it back?' Grandma rasped.

'Oh yes, but,' a slightly triumphant note crept into Flora's voice, 'I had a copy made.'

'And you've been coming up here.' It was more a statement than a question.

'Oh yes.'

'You know.'

'Yes, I know – but no one else. Nobody else.'

Jane and Sam might have been invisible – they froze, still as statues, not daring to move.

Flora started to cry again – piteous sobs wracking her body. She moved towards a cupboard, which was partly open.

'No!' Grandma shrieked. She raised her stick in a frenzy as if to bring it down on Flora, who shrank back but Sam leapt forward and wrenched the stick out of her cruel, claw-like hands. Stumbling against Flora, the pair fell in a confused heap against the cupboard door, which now slowly swung open. Like a flash of lightning, the brilliant contents were exposed, gleaming, glistening.

They all gazed silently, dazzled by the brightness.

In the distance, a foghorn groaned.

'I cleaned them for Father. I kept them clean, didn't I?' Flora's voice was high-pitched, querulous.

A huge silver crucifix stood at the centre, surrounded by intricately engraved silver candlesticks, chalices, huge silver vases, jugs, trays, plates, decorated boxes, silver bound volumes, delicately-wrought bowls with covers, ceremonial cups, goblets, all arrayed before them in a glittering display. Aladdin's cave . . . Treasure!

'I love beautiful things too, like Father. But he was wicked, wasn't he, Mother? Perhaps I am wicked too because I knew. I must hope to be forgiven.'

'Stop! Be quiet!' Grandma lunged towards her daughter, her face twisted with fury. 'Your father was the most highly respected, upright pillar of the community and the church . . .'

Flora began to laugh, softly at first, a chuckling sound rising to a hysterical cackle, far more frightening than all her sobs and moans. The protestations Grandma had been shrieking suddenly died. All her strength seemed to ebb away and before their eyes she crumpled – her normal imposing presence giving way to a shrunken wreck like a deflated balloon.

Jane knew suddenly what they were looking at. It's the church silver, the missing precious church silver. Stolen all those years ago – by Grandfather. His wife had known and had kept his secret . . . and so had Flora. Lucy's mother had found out and been silenced. And what about all the other stuff here and in the stable loft. Was it all loot?

At the same moment, Sam, too, suddenly understood everything.

'Stolen from the church,' he shouted, 'and my father was blamed. Out of work after that for the rest of his life. Killed 'im, it did. I'm off to fetch a bobby. I'm going to tell everyone – the whole world'll know.' He rushed towards the door.

Grandma, beyond words, put out a feeble shaking hand to stop him but he spat in her direction.

Jane raced after him, the sound of Flora's mad laughter following her down the stairs. 'I must go now . . . this minute.'

Sam had reached the front door. He turned briefly to look back. 'You coming?' She shook her head. 'Don't get lost in the fog,' she called.

'Good luck!' He waved, then was gone.

She guessed the dumb waiter would be in the kitchen and rushed downstairs. Yes, there it was. She climbed up inside beside the stars and moons box of tricks which Uncle Dolly had left behind and sat, squeezed into the small space. She closed her eyes. And then she remembered with horror. The little silver ball! Uncle Dolly's watch. She needed it desperately, without it she would be trapped here for ever. It had gone missing at the watch menders, which was where?

She eased herself out of the dumb waiter, feeling totally

forlorn and helpless, and walked back up to the hall. There was no sound now but she felt chilled at the thought of spending the night in the house with those two crazed women up in the tower. No good going out into the fog, getting lost, looking for a shop she didn't even know, which would be closed anyway. Her mind raced feverishly.

Someone was coming. She could hear stealthy footsteps but they were not coming down the main staircase. Jane froze. The door to the back stairs opened. She closed her eyes, not wanting to look. I'll have to make a run for it, out in the street, fog or no fog.

Then a woman's voice spoke – not Grandma's or Aunt Flora's. 'What you doing down here, love, at this time of night? And whatever's that you're wearing?'

Jane opened her eyes. By the hall lamp, she saw the parlour maid, Jessie, and she looked relieved.

'I heard a bit of a noise and thought I'd better see what was going on. The other two were snoring their heads off – dead to the world! Thought it might be a burglar so I brought this with me.' And she stood there in a long white nightdress brandishing a large candlestick.

No time for proper explanations, just something simple will do, Jane thought and said, 'Oh it was just Uncle Dolly leaving . . . going away.'

'Well, that's all right then. I'll get back to my warm bed and you ought to do the same, miss.' She turned to go, then said, 'Gone, has he? What a shame. A young boy from Jessops brought a small package round for him at tea-time, in this awful weather too, poor mite, he—'

'A small package? Where? I said I'd look after it for him. Where is it?' Jane asked frantically.

'Now, where did I put it? On the hall tray? No, I remember now, I popped it up on this shelf. Yes, here it is.' She reached up for the brown paper packet. Jane held her hands out.

'Catch!'

For a moment, the precious parcel – her future – hung in mid-air then landed safely in Jane's hands.

'Night, Jessie.'

'Up to bed with you now.' The back stairs door closed behind her.

She tore at the neat brown paper fastened with sealing wax. Inside was a box. Let it be the watch, please, let it be the watch, she prayed as she opened it.

There it was – a small silver globe. She picked it up carefully. Again, she pressed the tiny switch at the top and again it flew open to reveal the watch. She heard again the faint and haunting tune. The beautifully engraved writing she read again:

Backward, turn backward
O Time, in your flight . . .

Not backwards! Please not backwards!

There were a few more words, difficult to read. Holding it up to the lamp, she could just make out the words.

Forward, fast forward,
Just for one night.

Fast forward! Back quickly into the kitchen and back into the dumb waiter and, crouching there, she gripped the watch tightly and wound the switch forward as fast as she could, on and on until it felt as if a spring had broken but the fingers started to turn with a will of their own, faster and faster. Staring at them in the dimness, she became dizzy, mesmerised by them. Round and round they twirled. Now she was whirling and circling up and up, as if she would fly out of the top of the kitchen, the dining room, bedrooms, the roof of the house and go spiralling crazily up to the moon and infinity. Just when she felt the top of her head would lift off, the spinning came to an abrupt stop. She was flung roughly sideways, banging her head, and was violently sick. Billa's coat taking the worst of it.

Dazed, with her stomach still churning and head throbbing, she stayed still for a minute with her eyes closed. She felt as if she might be sick again, then the feeling passed. Cautiously, she opened her eyes. Things had stopped going round and had steadied.

She touched the sliding door and gingerly pushed it back, hardly daring to look through.

It seemed lighter. It was an untidy room into which she crawled down, full of books, papers, clothes lying scattered on every surface. It certainly wasn't the night-time kitchen she'd left but, despite the chaos, it couldn't have looked more beautiful to Jane.

'Billa's room!' she shouted aloud.

Not the formal dining room any more, with its polished mahogany table, gleaming silver and velvet curtains – all the grandeur, the hypocrisy, the pretensions, that had all gone, vanished. All collapsed like a house of cards. Shaky foundations, then it collapsed, she thought simply.

The room was still freezing and Billa's coat offered no snugness. The matted strands of fur were damp and now stinking.

'She'll kill me!'

Skirting her way through piles of clutter, she opened the door and went into the hall, looking round curiously. It was familiar and yet strange. The small cloakroom had been contrived out of part of the old back stairs, which had led down to the kitchen, and she thought briefly of Jessie, Mrs Murphy and Ivy, while she scrubbed fiercely at the coat in cold water – no luxury of warm water here. She carried it, still dripping, back across the hall, and met Shannon, who was in a hurry.

'Hi. Everything OK?' he asked.

She was so glad to see him. Thankful that it wasn't just the present house that had come back.

'Settling in all right? It's a great house, isn't it? Real shame that it's going to be turned into' – he put on a posh voice here – 'stunning apartments and we'll all have to go and live in halls of residence. In other words – little boxes. Ah well, that's life and modern times. What's happened to the cat, by the way?' He gestured at the coat then rushed on out of the front door.

She draped the coat over a broken chair and caught sight of herself in the yellowed cracked mirror.

'I look terrible.'

So much has happened here. She thought of all the people who'd lived in the house, how she'd envied their secure, well-ordered lives. But it had all been a fake, an illusion, just like one of Uncle Dolly's tricks, and had disappeared and hey presto, bazooka! the whole set up had gone, vanished.

Whatever had become of Uncle Dolly – had he become a celebrity of the London stage? And Aunt Lallie – caught up in a life of marches and demonstrations? Poor guilt-ridden Flora – a convent for her, perhaps. Had she even survived? Had Grandma? Perhaps the demented woman would have been locked up in the same institution where Lucy's mother had been shut away – and serve her right. She hoped Sam had managed to change his life around, and Henry . . . but most of all Lucy . . . what had . . .

The front door slammed. There was a buzz in the hall now – sounds of people laughing, shouting, running up the stairs.

Billa came into the room and dumped a bulging bag on the floor.

'Billa!' Jane threw herself on to her sister and hugged her.

'What's all the fuss?' Billa looked at her sister critically. 'You look terrible – and what on earth have you done to your hair?'

She suddenly caught sight of her coat.

'I don't believe it, I do not believe it!' she screamed. She picked it up. 'It's soaking . . . and it stinks!'

'I'm really, really sorry. It'll wash up all right. Some strong detergent—'

'Wash! It'll have to be dry cleaned and how on earth can I afford that? There's a dry cleaner's in the Old Music Hall shopping arcade, a few streets away – next to an Oxfam and you can pay for it.'

'I've got seven pounds left from some money Mum gave me.'

'That might cover it. And talking of Mum, she sent a message for you on my mobile – she didn't get the job in Weston Super Mare and she's decided to go up to Scotland – some fish factory in Aberdeen, something like that. Anyway, the point is,' she looked at Jane and her expression softened slightly, 'she wants to know, if you want to go with her or . . . or go to Dad.'

'I'll stay with Mum,' Jane said firmly. Mum, who was honest . . . too honest sometimes. It might be tough at times but they'd talk things through, work things out. There was no need to conceal anything with Mum – no need for secrets.

'So that's sorted then. Now, about supper – no need for us to bother tonight. Izzy's asked us for a meal. She does fantastic Italian. Her spag. bol – mmmmm.' Billa closed her eyes expressively to make her point. 'She lives at the very top of the house with Karl and Eb – bit of a climb up – they call it the Tower Room and they swear it's haunted. Scary eh?'